As he reached the open doorway,
Stephen saw Jill approaching.

Backlit by sunlight, he couldn't see the expression on her face. She stopped when she saw him. Before she could react, he reached out and grabbed her arm.

"Why?" he said through clenched teeth. "Why didn't you tell me?"

Her whole body trembled. "T-tell you what?"

"Don't play innocent with me, Jill. I know Jordan is my son. And you had no right to keep that from me. No right at all."

He thought she would continue to deny it, but she didn't. She just looked at him. Tears glistened in her eyes. The sunlight pouring into the barn lit her hair from behind, giving the impression of a halo. But this was no angel standing there.

This was a warm-blooded, sexy woman—and the mother of his child.

"I'm so sorry," she whispered.

For a moment Stephen wasn't sure what he wanted more: to kiss her or shake her. The desire to kiss her won out, and he yanked her into his arms and covered her mouth with his own.

Dear Reader,

This book was truly a labor of love. I got the idea several years ago and it simply would not let me go. Finally I decided to see if I couldn't figure out a way to tell the story so that it could have a happy ending, for that was the problem. In my head, I could see the story going so far and then no farther. But eventually all fell into place, and *His Brother's Bride-To-Be* was born.

There were other problems besides the elusive happy ending. For one, I was setting the story on a ranch and I know absolutely zero about ranches, even though I live in Texas. Second problem was my complete lack of knowledge about horses. But these two problems were easily solved since my two critique partners are both avid horsewomen and were able to supply the background information I was missing. So a hearty thank-you goes to Alaina Richardson and Colleen Thompson. I don't know what I'd do without you.

I love to hear from readers. Please visit me at www.patriciakay.com and drop me a line. I promise to write back.

Happy reading!

Patricia Kay

This book is dedicated, with love,
to all the wonderful readers who have written to me over
the years. Your letters and e-mails have meant so much.
Knowing that my books have brightened your lives or
helped you through a bad time is a gift I will always
treasure. Thank you from the bottom of my heart.

PATRICIA KAY

Formerly writing as Trisha Alexander, Patricia Kay is a *USA TODAY*-bestselling author of more than thirty contemporary romances. She lives in Houston, Texas. To learn more about her, visit her Web site at www.patriciakay.com.

Chapter One

Stephen Wells winced when he heard the unmistakable ring of his cell phone. *Dammit.* He'd meant to turn the blasted thing off before entering Jake Burrow's office because he knew how much the old man hated interruptions. He especially hated cell phones.

Sure enough, Jake glared.

"Sorry," Stephen said, digging the phone out of his pocket. He was about to switch it off when he saw the number displayed. *Caroline?* Giving Jake an apologetic look and a murmured, "I'll just be a minute," Stephen rose and walked out of the office.

"Hello?"

"Stephen? Thank God I found you."

Although she was a year older than him, Caroline was his niece, the daughter of his older half-brother, Elliott. Stephen could hear the barely concealed panic

in her voice, and he froze. All he could think was that
something had happened to Elliott. "What's wrong?"

"It's Daddy."

Stephen couldn't breathe.

"You're not going to believe this, Stephen. He's getting
married!" With each word, her voice climbed higher.

Stephen blinked. Married? *Elliott?* That was impossible. "Where did you get that idea? Just who is he
supposed to be marrying?" She had to be mistaken. To
Stephen's knowledge, Elliott hadn't even dated anyone
since the death of his wife fourteen months earlier.

"Where do you *think* I got that idea? From him! He
called not five minutes ago to say he's bringing this
woman home with him."

"I don't—"

"And that's not all. She's younger than *me!*" Once
again, her voice had climbed.

"Younger than *you?*" Caroline was thirty-four. Elliott
was fifty-seven. "How do you know that?"

"Because Dad *told* me. Oh, he didn't volunteer the
information. I had to dig it out of him. And trust me, he
wasn't too keen about admitting it, either."

Stephen didn't know what to say.

"She's obviously a gold digger," Caroline said bitterly.

"Oh, c'mon, you're jumping to conclusions." But
Stephen's mind was spinning. When could Elliott have
met this woman? And where? And why hadn't he mentioned her to Stephen? "Just who is she, do you know?"

"Somebody he met on one of his business trips to
Austin." Austin was a five-hour drive from their southwest Texas ranch and Elliott, who had myriad business
interests, traveled there often.

"Well, I'll be damned," Stephen said softly. He'd known his brother was lonely since Adele's death. Stephen missed her, too—she'd been a wonderful person—so he could imagine how Elliott felt. But…getting married? And so soon? To a woman so young? Stephen wanted to believe Elliott knew what he was doing, that this woman was worthy of his brother, that Elliott's considerable fortune had had nothing to do with her willingness to become the second Mrs. Lawrence. Yet even as Stephen speculated, he felt guilty. Elliott was a good-looking, virile man in terrific shape. And fifty-seven wasn't old by a long shot.

"You've got to come home, Stephen. He's bringing her here tomorrow."

"I can't be there tomorrow. I'll be back on Saturday."

"I want you to be here when they get here. I'm going to need the moral support."

"Look, Caroline, what's the difference? Me being there or not being there? It's not like they're getting married tomorrow. Besides—"

"Besides, what?"

Stephen wanted to say his loyalty and sympathy lay with Elliott. If anyone deserved to be happy, it was him. But Stephen knew better. Caroline was upset enough. No sense making things worse. He chose his words carefully. "I just think we should reserve our judgment. Give your dad a break, you know?"

"A break! He's obviously lost his mind! Anyway, I haven't told you everything. She's got a son. A *son!* And from what Dad said, he's younger than *Tyler.*" Tyler was Caroline's son. "I'm telling you, you've *got* to be here. You're the one Dad listens to." This last was said with an undertone of resentment.

Stephen stifled a sigh. He knew Caroline would give him no peace until he capitulated. And the truth was, he did think it might be a good idea to be there when Elliott and the woman and her son arrived, if only to act as a buffer between Caroline and the happy couple. Maybe he could seal the deal on the filly with Jake quickly and leave for home early in the morning. "All right," he said with resignation, "I'll do my best."

But it took until noon the following day before the registration papers for the filly were ready and all the arrangements were made to ship the quarter horse out to the ranch the following week. Caroline hadn't been happy when Stephen called to tell her it was impossible for him to get there before late afternoon.

But it couldn't be helped. The filly was too promising—they planned to use her specifically for breeding stock—for Stephen to walk away. He had a job to do, and no matter what Caroline wanted, he had to finish it before he could even think about going home.

At least he would make it back before dark. Stephen was certified on instruments, but he preferred to fly in the daylight, when he could see. Thinking about the Cessna 152 two-seater he'd purchased the previous year, he couldn't help smiling. Stephen had fallen in love with flying during his first year of law school at Harvard. He'd shared an apartment with a flying enthusiast from Connecticut and had quickly gotten hooked himself.

After renting planes for years, he'd finally decided to make the leap and buy his own. He'd been afraid Elliott would disapprove and try to talk him out of it, but his brother had encouraged him, even though Elliott was a white-knuckle flier himself who preferred to get around by walking, riding his beloved horses, or driving one of his two trucks.

Stephen frowned. Elliott meant more to him than anyone on the face of the earth. He would, literally, lie down and die for his brother. He sure hoped Caroline was wrong and that this woman Elliott planned to marry truly loved him. Yet he couldn't help but worry.

Because even if the woman turned out to be wonderful, Stephen knew Caroline could make life miserable for her. Which would, in turn, make life miserable for Elliott.

And me....

Much of this and other problems would be lessened if Caroline had a place of her own. Even Elliott realized that, but he was too softhearted where his daughter was concerned to do anything about it. The trouble was, he'd encouraged her to move back to the ranch after her divorce four years ago, and now that Adele was gone nothing short of an earthquake would dislodge her. Even if she *had* been inclined to find a separate home for herself and her son, this new development would cause her to dig her heels even deeper.

Because if there was one thing you could count on, it was Caroline's fierce possessiveness where her father was concerned. This obsession, this need to be number one in her father's life, had begun when she was little, "the princess," the spoiled only child of parents who had wanted more children but were unable to have them so lavished all their attention and love on their daughter. It was the source of all the friction between Stephen and Caroline, for she was intensely jealous of the relationship between the two brothers. It was a measure of how upset she was over Elliott's engagement that she had called Stephen about it, for normally he would be the last person she'd turn to.

Stephen heaved a sigh.

He smelled big trouble ahead.

"Don't worry, darling. Everything's going to be fine, you'll see."

Jill Emerson smiled at her fiancé. Elliott was such a sweetheart. She had never believed she would ever find a man like him. Considerate, thoughtful, kind, loving... He was just all around terrific, and she was a lucky woman.

But despite Elliott's assurance, she wasn't sure every-thing *would* be fine. She'd seen the look on his face after he'd finished talking to his daughter and telling her about their coming marriage. He'd admitted afterward that Caroline was "a little upset" but had assured Jill that she'd get over it. "It's just that she didn't expect this," he'd added. "I should have told her about you months ago."

Caroline's reaction was much stronger than he'd let on, Jill suspected. He just didn't want Jill to worry. Truth was, Jill understood how Elliott's daughter must feel. Elliott had told Jill that Caroline had been very close to her mother. She was bound to be upset that her father wanted to marry again so soon.

Plus there's the age difference.

Elliott was fifty-seven, and Jill was thirty. To many people this would have been an insurmountable obstacle to the relationship, but the difference in their ages didn't bother Jill at all.

But Caroline couldn't know that. She probably imagined Jill was only interested in Elliott's money. After all, how was she to know that Jill loved Elliott and would have agreed to marry him even if he wasn't wealthy—something Jill hadn't known when she'd first started seeing him.

Jill actually liked the fact Elliott was more mature. Older men were more responsible and committed, she'd found. Plus they had confidence and didn't constantly need propping up. Not that Jill had had that much experience with men of any age. In the past ten years she'd been too busy finishing college, and caring for her terminally ill aunt, as well as raising Jordan and supporting both of them after her aunt's death, to have much time for anything else.

As if he knew her thoughts had turned to him, Jordan removed his headphones and said, "Elliott, when are we going to be there?"

Jill and Elliott exchanged amused smiles. Although Elliott still didn't know Jordan the way Jill did, he'd known him long enough to realize the ten-year-old was long on curiosity but short on patience.

"It'll be another hour or so, son," Elliott said.

Jordan heaved a noisy sigh. "Okay."

"How about if we stop for some ice cream?" Elliott suggested. "There's a store right up the road that sells the best homemade ice cream you've ever tasted."

"Will ice cream make the time go faster?" Jill teased.

"As far as I'm concerned, good ice cream solves all the world's problems," Elliott said, winking at her.

The funny thing was, the ice cream *did* seem to make the remainder of the trip go faster—not that Jill was in any hurry to get there. But she knew Jordan was tired of being in the car and Elliott was anxious to get home.

"We're almost there now," Elliott said. "When we get to the top of that rise, you'll be able to see the ranch."

Jill smiled, even though inside she was a mass of nerves. *I've made the right decision,* she told herself yet again. *I do love Elliott, and Jordan adores him. That's what counts. If his family is suspicious, they have a right to be. I'll just have to show them I'm not a threat. And I've got the entire summer to win them over.*

She'd made it clear to Elliott that she wouldn't marry him until September, even though he'd wanted the wedding to take place immediately. She simply had to be sure his family would welcome her and Jordan. Accepting anything less would be unfair, not just to him but to all of them. Although Elliott had been disappointed, he hadn't pushed once he realized she'd made up her mind. The one thing he *had* said, though, was that he knew it would be uncomfortable for her if Caroline remained at the ranch after the wedding.

"We'll talk about her finding her own place," Elliott had promised.

"Don't do anything right away," Jill had answered. "Let's just see how things go."

Breaking into her thoughts now, Elliott said, "There it is."

The quiet pride in his voice warmed Jill. His love of home and family was one of his greatest attractions for her, a quality that had shone through even on their first meeting. Remembering that Saturday in January made Jill forget her reservations and smile again.

Elliott had come into the small gallery where Jill's paintings were sold and where she worked several afternoons a week and most weekends. He was looking for a birthday present for his daughter, he said. Jill had immediately liked him: his kind blue eyes, the warmth of his smile and the attentive way he listened as she explained the merits of the different pieces that interested him.

He'd settled on one of her favorite paintings—a delicate watercolor of one of the old missions near her aunt's home in San Marcos.

"I hope your daughter likes this," she'd said as she wrapped the painting.

"I'm sure she will," he said. "All of your paintings are beautiful."

Just then Jordan had burst through the front door. On the days she worked there, she'd arranged for him to get a ride to the gallery after school, not only because hiring a babysitter to watch him until Jill got home would have strained her budget to a frightening point, but because Jill liked having him there.

He sat in the small office in the back and did his homework while having a snack; Jill's friend and employer, Nora O'Malley, always kept fruit and drinks in the refrigerator for him. When he finished, Jill would allow him to turn on the small TV back there, but she never let him watch more than an hour's worth of Animal Planet, his favorite channel. Instead she encouraged him to read.

Thinking about how Elliott had immediately shown interest in Jordan, and Jordan in him, Jill felt blessed. It seemed like a miracle that she'd found this man, who not only loved her but also loved her son.

Even so, she hadn't been sure about marrying him. When he'd first asked her, a month ago, she hadn't immediately said yes. Instead she'd told him how honored she was that he wanted her for his wife, but that she'd need some time to think about it. "There are so many things to consider," she'd said.

"I understand," he'd answered before she'd had the chance to say anything more. "Take all the time you need."

That was another of his wonderful qualities. He had true empathy for people and seemed able to always place himself in their shoes. This was a rare trait in anyone, and Jill knew it. But still she'd hesitated. Marrying Elliott would bring about monumental changes in her life and in Jordan's. She would have to give up her teaching post as a traveling art teacher between several Austin schools as well as her job at the gallery, and she would be leaving everything familiar—her friends, her church, her career—and going into the unknown.

"I wouldn't hesitate for a minute," Nora had said. "He's a catch, Jill. In fact, if you don't want him, I'm going after him!"

She'd laughed when she said it, but Jill knew Nora was more than halfway serious.

"Besides," Nora had added, "you can paint anywhere. And I'll always be happy to sell your work, you know that."

But the deciding factor in Jill's accepting Elliott's proposal came from Jordan. He'd been delighted when Jill told him she might marry Elliott, that they might move to Elliott's ranch.

"Cool!" he'd said, his eyes lighting up with excitement. "Maybe Elliott'll get me a horse!"

When she'd told Elliott her decision, he'd said she made him the happiest man on earth and that she would never be sorry. With those words, her last lingering doubts slipped away.

I am very lucky, she thought now, *so no matter what it takes, no matter how hard I have to work at it, I will do everything in my power to win over both Caroline and his brother. Because Elliott and Jordan deserve no less.*

Caroline Lawrence Conway paced the living room of her father's ranch house. Her heels hammered against the hardwood floors. If her father had been there, he'd have frowned. He didn't like her wearing spike heels when walking on his precious wood, and normally Caroline wanted nothing more than to please her father. But right then, she didn't care what he would think if he saw her.

How *could* he call from out of the blue and tell her he was engaged? To a woman they didn't know and that he'd never mentioned? One who was even younger than Caroline herself? It was horrible. Sickening. Disgusting. Why, her mother had only been dead fourteen months! She was barely cold in her grave. Their friends would be scandalized. They'd think her father, who'd always been so sensible, had lost his mind.

Furious tears filled Caroline's eyes. She couldn't believe this had happened. Once again, she replayed the conversation with her father.

"Hello, princess," he'd said. "Just wanted you to know I'll be back tomorrow afternoon."

Caroline had smiled. She missed her father when he wasn't there. "What would you like for dinner? Want me to thaw out some steaks? And I'll ask Marisol to make that potato and cheese casserole you like so much."

"That sounds perfect," he'd said. "But take out an extra steak or two. I'm bringing a couple of people with me."

"Oh?" She still hadn't suspected a thing. She'd thought he meant business associates—a new contact, perhaps.

"I wanted you to be the first to know, Caroline. I'm…engaged to be married."

Caroline had been so shocked, she'd been unable to speak. Then she'd thought she'd misunderstood him. "Wh-what did you say?"

He'd laughed. "I said, I'm engaged. Her name is Jill. And she has a ten-year-old son named Jordan. They're both coming home with me tomorrow. I can't wait for you to meet her."

After that, Caroline wasn't sure *what* she'd said. She'd been shaking and very upset. She hadn't even tried to hide it. And her father, who was normally the kindest of men, had acted as if he were oblivious. He'd just said, "I know you're going to love Jill, Caroline. I think you'll be the best of friends."

Finally she'd recovered enough to ask questions, which he'd reluctantly answered. That was when she'd found out how young his new fiancée was.

Thinking about that now, Caroline knew he'd hoped to wait until he got home before he'd have to admit that he planned to marry a woman younger than his own daughter. That the woman, this *Jill* person, was a gold digger was a given.

Yes, Caroline knew her father was handsome, but he was fifty-seven years old, for crying out loud! Maybe fifty-seven-year-old movie stars married thirty-year-old women, but in the real world, that didn't happen unless the man was wealthy. And ever since oil had been discovered on their land, Elliott Tyler Lawrence had become extremely wealthy.

Oh, this woman was after his money, no doubt about it. She'd taken one look at Caroline's father and seen a permanent meal ticket. Honestly, men were such *fools,* Caroline thought bitterly.

She could just imagine what this Jill looked like. She was probably a big-breasted, blond, Pamela Anderson type. Friends! Was her father *serious?* There was no way on God's green earth that Caroline would *ever* become friends with some slut who was trying to usurp Caroline's mother's rightful place in her father's heart.

And *mine.*

Frightened tears welled in Caroline's eyes. How *could* he?

"Miss Caroline?"

Caroline whirled around. Marisol, their longtime housekeeper, stood in the arched doorway that led into the main foyer of the large ranch house. She was wiping her hands on her ever-present apron.

"What is it, Marisol?"

"For dessert tonight, Miss Caroline? I thought I'd make flan. Is that all right with you?"

"I don't care. Whatever you want to make."

After the housekeeper turned to go back to the kitchen, Caroline walked to the front window. She angrily swiped at her eyes, then gazed out at the bright June day. She was afraid to think about what would happen if her dad's marriage plans went through. Would he want Caroline and Tyler to move? What would she do if he did? Just the idea of having to be out on her own again made her feel sick.

I can't. I won't.

She was still thinking of the possible consequences of her father's news when she spied his dark red Dodge Ram truck at the top of the rise that led to the main house. Her heartbeat quickened. She was glad they were here early, before Tyler got home from his friend Evan's house.

Thinking about her twelve-year-old son and the last thing her father had said to her before they'd hung up yesterday, she clenched her teeth. He thought Tyler and that woman's *brat* would be friends, too. Huh. Not if Caroline had anything to say about it, they wouldn't.

Taking a deep breath and stiffening her spine, she stalked out to the foyer and yanked open the door.

Chapter Two

Jill, nervous but trying to look as if she wasn't, watched as Elliott, with a big smile on his face, walked over to meet the cool-looking blonde standing in the open doorway. She wore slim-cut jeans, layered tank tops in plum and white, and what looked like four-inch heels. She was very thin, almost brittle-looking. Her grayish-blue eyes held not a hint of warmth as they swept over Jill and Jordan.

Jill swallowed, and her heartbeat accelerated. She told herself she was a grown woman, that she shouldn't be intimidated by Elliott's daughter, that Rome wasn't built in a day and that, given time, she would win Caroline over.

"Hello, sweetheart," Elliott said, giving Caroline a hug.

She returned his hug, but her attention remained riveted on Jill and Jordan. Elliott reached for Jill's hand

and led her forward. "Caroline, this is Jill…and this handsome guy is Jordan."

"Hello, Caroline," Jill said. She projected the warmest smile she could muster. "It's so nice to meet you." She stuck her hand out. "Elliott's told me so much about you." She immediately wished she could take the last words back; she almost expected Caroline to answer, *Well, he told me nothing about you!*

"Hi," piped Jordan, blue eyes bright with curiosity.

"Hello," Caroline said. She didn't smile in return, and for a moment it looked as if she would ignore Jill's hand, too, but she finally gave it a brief shake.

To fill the awkward silence, Jill looked around. "It's so beautiful here." The rolling landscape dotted with shrubs and wildflowers, the river a few hundred yards away, the distant hills, the endless blue sky—Jill already itched to capture the scene with paint.

"Not as beautiful as it used to be," Elliott said ruefully.

Jill knew he hated what he called the invasion of the oil derricks, although from here only the myriad buildings that were part of the working life of the ranch were visible. He'd told her the derricks and other equipment associated with the drilling operation were concentrated in the northwest quadrant of his property, which was very large—some thirty-two thousand acres in all.

"Where are the horses, Elliott?" Jordan said.

"I'll take you over to the stables to see them after we get you and your mother settled in," Elliott said, grinning at him. Putting his arm around Jill, he added, "Now that you've met Caroline, I'll drive you around to the guesthouse, okay?"

"Okay," Jill said, doubly grateful, now that she'd

met Caroline, that she would have her own private place here.

Throughout this exchange, Caroline had said nothing. Turning his gaze back to his daughter, Elliott said, "Caroline, tell Marisol we probably won't want dinner before eight. We ate a late lunch."

"Eight?" She seemed about to protest, but finally just shrugged. "Marisol won't like it."

"Marisol will be fine with it," Elliott said firmly. His tone brooked no further discussion.

Jill didn't know where to look. Caroline's attitude told her more clearly than words that Jill had her work cut out for her if she hoped to win over Elliott's daughter. In fact, the situation was even worse than Jill had imagined. Caroline wasn't just wary or reserving her opinion of Jill until she'd had a chance to get to know her. It was obvious she considered Jill an enemy.

She hates me.

Jill bit her lip. She knew Elliott would say she was attaching far too much importance to Caroline's actions today, but she didn't think so.

Maybe I should have let Elliott ask her to move. Because unless I can win her over quickly, I'm not sure the two of us can survive here together, even for the summer.

By now Jill and Elliott and Jordan had piled back into the truck and Elliott drove around to the back of the house where Jill saw another house—this one a small frame cottage sitting about sixty feet away, close to the bank of the river. The cottage was painted pale yellow, with red shutters. It even had a front porch with a swing. It was utterly charming.

"Oh," Jill said. "Elliott, it's so pretty." She was delighted, and when Elliott unlocked the front door and they walked inside, she was even more delighted.

They entered a kitchen/living room combination. Branching off from this main room were two bedrooms, a good-size bathroom with both tub and walk-in shower, and a sunporch that faced the river. The entire house was warm and hospitable, filled with solid maple furniture, lots of chintz, hardwood floors, and bright area rugs.

"This is the main bedroom," Elliott said, opening the door to an inviting room with a queen-size bed, a rocking chair, a small desk, and a matching walnut dresser and chest of drawers.

"And this will be Jordan's room." Grinning, Elliott opened the other door.

"Oh, Elliott," Jill said when she saw the maple bunk beds, the matching chest of drawers and desk, the laptop computer, the TV set, and the bookcases half-filled with books.

"Cool!" Jordan said. He immediately plopped down at the desk and opened the computer. "Is this mine?" he asked excitedly.

"It certainly is."

"Awesome!"

Jill rolled her eyes. The words *cool* and *awesome* seemed to be the only ones in Jordan's vocabulary right now. "Elliott," she murmured. "You shouldn't have." She tried to quash the guilt she felt over his generosity, and she was only partially successful.

"Except for the TV and computer, most of this stuff came from the room Stephen used as a boy."

The half brother. "Does he live on the ranch, too?"

"Not anymore. A few months ago he bought a place in town. This used to be his house, you know."

"Oh, I didn't realize…" Then a thought struck her. "He didn't move because of *me,* did he?"

"No, of course not. He doesn't even know about you yet." He smiled. "You'll meet him tomorrow."

Another hurdle to face, Jill thought in trepidation. If Elliott's brother hated her, too, life here at the ranch really would be unbearable for her.

I've got to win them over. I've simply got to. Because if I don't, I won't have a choice. Marriage to Elliott will be impossible.

Stephen's pre-flight routine was set. Carefully following a checklist, he went over the interior of the plane to make sure all switches were off and the parking brake was set. From there, he examined both sides of the airplane to make sure there was no external damage. In the back, he looked at the hinges, nuts and bolts, then studied the general condition of the rudder, the elevator and the stabilizer. Next came the flaps and ailerons, then the tires and wheels, the landing gear and the brake lines.

When he reached the fuel tank, he took off the cap and checked the fuel level. After that, he opened the cowling, checked the oil level and all the hoses and wires. He carefully examined the engine, the throttles, the spark plugs. As he checked each item, he marked it off his list.

The first time Elliott had watched Stephen do all this he'd said, "Do you think something's wrong?" His inference was that something must be wrong if Stephen had to inspect so many things.

Stephen had just smiled. "No, but thorough checks of everything before you get up in the air prevents problems. It's the main reason flying is so safe."

Elliott had nodded, reassured.

Today Stephen found everything in order, and after loading his gear and receiving the okay from the tower, he taxied to the lone runway of the small county airport and was soon in the air. It was a gorgeous summer afternoon, with clear skies—perfect flying weather.

After climbing at fifty-five knots to his cruising altitude of ten thousand feet, Stephen kept his air speed at a hundred knots and settled back to enjoy the flight. He figured he'd get to McPherson's, the private airport where he kept his plane, in less than an hour and a half, which would put him at the ranch about five.

He wondered if he should have called Elliott to tell him he'd be back earlier than planned. Then again, what did it matter? Elliott wouldn't care.

For the rest of the uneventful flight, Stephen thought about Elliott and how much he owed him. Stephen had been only five years old when his parents—his and Elliott's mother, Felicia, and her second husband, Stephen Alexander Wells, for whom Stephen had been named—had been killed in an automobile accident while on vacation in England where they'd been visiting friends. Elliott and Adele had taken Stephen in, and made him feel loved and secure.

Caroline had even been happy; she'd been six, and although she was spoiled, she liked having Stephen to boss around and play with. It had only been later, when she decided her father was spending too much time with

Stephen, that he might even prefer Stephen over her, that she'd become so possessive and contentious.

Most of the time, Stephen ignored her. He let her comments roll right off him. Sticks and stones, he'd told himself. Besides, going into battle with her would only have upset Elliott and wouldn't have changed a thing.

But today, thinking about the past twenty-eight years, Stephen made a vow. If he saw that this new intended wife of Elliott's was the real deal and that his brother was truly happy, he would do everything possible to make sure Caroline didn't spoil things. If, on the other hand, Caroline was right and the fiancée really was a gold digger, then he might have to join forces with Caroline to drive the woman off.

It was almost four-thirty before he landed, a half hour later than he'd hoped to arrive. Torn between going to his house first so he could have a quick shower and a change of clothes before dinner, and seeing Elliott first, he decided he'd go home and simply give Elliott a call telling him he was there.

"Stephen!" Elliott said. "I thought you weren't coming back till tomorrow."

"I finished up early." Stephen gave his brother a quick rundown on his trip, then said, "Caroline told me your news."

"I'm sure she did." Then Elliott's voice lightened. "I can't wait for you to meet Jill. Were you planning to come out for dinner?"

"If you want me." *Jill. So that's her name.*

"Of course I want you. Bring Emily, too." Stephen had been dating Emily Lindstrom, who owned a dance studio in High Creek, for the past year.

"Emily's still in Sweden. She won't be back until Saturday afternoon."

"If she's not too tired, bring her out Saturday night, then. I thought I'd have a small party to introduce Jill to our friends."

"Okay. What time do you want me tonight?"

"Dinner's at eight. But come to the house early. We'll have drinks and talk."

"I'm looking forward to it. I have to admit, I was surprised about your engagement. You're a sly fox. You never said a word."

"I know. I'm sorry. But I... Well, I wasn't sure about Jill and I wanted to wait until I was."

"Oh?" *So Elliott had his own doubts about the woman. That doesn't sound good.*

"No, it's not what you think. I was always sure about *my* feelings for her. What I wasn't sure about were hers for me. And I didn't want anyone feeling sorry for me if she said no when I asked her to marry me."

"I see."

"Listen, when you meet her, you'll understand." His voice softened. "She's wonderful, Stephen. I keep pinching myself. I still can't believe she loves me."

She'd better love you. She'd better not be the kind of woman Caroline thinks she is. "Tell me about her. How'd you meet her? And when?"

"It was on a trip to Austin in January. I—" Abruptly, he broke off. "What are you doing now?"

"I was thinking about taking a shower."

"How about if I take a run into town? I'd rather talk to you in person."

"Sounds good."

Stephen took a quick shower and by the time he'd changed into khakis and a dark blue shirt, Elliott had arrived. The brothers hugged—something they did whether they'd been apart months or just days.

"Want a beer?" Stephen asked, heading for his small kitchen.

"Sure." Elliott sat on one end of the black leather sectional sofa that took up the major part of Stephen's living room.

Rejoining him a few seconds later, Stephen handed him a cold Dos Equis and sat across from him. "Now, tell me all about her."

Elliott's smile lit his entire face. "She's special, Stephen. Really special. You'll see. The moment I set eyes on her, I knew it."

It gave Stephen pause to see how happy his brother looked. He hadn't looked this happy since before Adele got sick. Jesus, he would kill this Jill if she hurt Elliott.

Stephen listened quietly as Elliott told him how he'd been walking from his hotel to a nearby restaurant during one of his business trips to Austin and how he'd spied this watercolor painting in the window of a gallery and how it had immediately caught his eye. "You know, the one I gave Caroline for her birthday. The mission."

Stephen nodded. He *did* remember. He'd really liked the painting himself.

"It's Jill's painting," Elliott said proudly. "When I went into the gallery to inquire about it, she was working there. She sold it to me."

"So she's an artist?"

"Among other things. She also teaches art at several

elementary schools—well, she did. She gave her notice last week. She's really talented."

For some reason, that information made Stephen feel better about the unknown Jill. Although he knew a teacher could be just as devious as anyone else, at least she'd been working in a respectable profession.

"Anyway, she's wonderful. I never believed in love at first sight, but that's exactly what happened." Elliott smiled sheepishly. "You probably think it's ridiculous…a man of my age acting like a lovesick kid."

"Of course it's not ridiculous. And what do you mean, *a man of my age?* Hell, you're in the prime of your life, Elliott."

Elliott hesitated. "She's a lot younger than I am." His voice turned defensive. "She's only thirty."

"I know."

"You do?"

"Caroline also told me that."

Elliott's expression changed. He sighed. "Caroline."

"She's not happy."

"I know she's not, but she'll have to get over it," Elliott said firmly. "Because Jill is here and I intend to marry her. We're planning a September wedding."

Stephen wanted to ask what they were waiting for if this Jill had already quit her job, but he decided he'd better not look a gift horse in the mouth. After all, if he determined the woman was bad news, at least he'd have some time. To do what, he wasn't sure. All he knew was that he'd do whatever it took to keep his brother from being hurt.

A knock woke Jill, who had stretched out for a nap after unpacking. Rubbing her eyes, she glanced at the clock on the bedside table. Six-thirty! Jumping up, she walked out to the living room and opened the door.

"I was just about to call out the cavalry," Elliott said, grinning. "I knocked a couple of times." He looked fresh—he'd obviously showered—and had changed into gray dress slacks and an open-necked white shirt. His salt-and-pepper hair was still wet and his blue eyes shone with love as he studied her.

Jill made a face. "I fell asleep." She pushed a strand of hair away from her face. She could just imagine how rumpled and messy she looked.

"You must have needed it. I just came to tell you that after you've had a chance to freshen up, you should come over to the main house. We'll have a drink and you can meet Stephen."

"Stephen? I thought you said he wasn't coming home until tomorrow."

"He finished his business early, so he flew home this afternoon. He's looking forward to meeting you."

I'll just bet he is… As soon as the thought formed, Jill was ashamed of herself. She had no right to judge Elliott's brother before she'd even met him. Just because Caroline had behaved as if Jill were a viper didn't mean he would.

"You'll like him, sweetheart."

Jill smiled gratefully. Elliott was such a dear. "I'm sure I will."

Elliott gave her a shoulder hug. "Now, go on. Get ready."

"Before I do, do you know where Jordan is?" She felt guilty for completely abandoning him.

"He's fine, Jill. Quit worrying. He and Tyler are playing a video game. And before you ask, I showed

him all over the parts of the ranch within walking
distance—warned him what might be dangerous, what
he shouldn't touch, where he shouldn't go unless I
was with him."

Giving her a kiss on the cheek, Elliott left her then,
and Jill headed toward the bathroom.

She knew she was only postponing the inevitable,
but she drew a bath and stayed in the tub as long as
she possibly could, then took an even longer time
dressing and putting on her makeup. When she was
finished, she inspected herself in the mirror. She'd
chosen a silky cream-and-russet-print skirt and
matching russet summer-weight sweater that compli-
mented her hair and hazel eyes. She'd kept her makeup
subtle—just a touch of mascara, faint taupe eye
shadow, lipstick in a shade called Nectarine—and her
hairstyle simple. Non-threatening, she told herself in
a flash of brief amusement.

Suddenly, she was mad at herself for stalling. *Don't
be a wimp. Get out there. Put your head up in the air
and walk into that room proudly. You have nothing to
be ashamed of. You love Elliott, and he loves you.*

She heard low male voices as she entered the house.
The voices stopped when her footsteps drew near.

Taking a deep breath, Jill entered the living room.

"Darling!" Elliott jumped up from one of the sofas
in front of the fireplace and walked over to her.

Another man stood, too.

"Come meet my brother," Elliott said, taking her arm
and leading her forward. His voice rang with pride as
he made the introductions. "Jill, this is my brother,
Stephen. Stephen, this is Jill."

Jill turned and got her first good look at Elliott's brother, who was tall, with thick brown hair and deep blue eyes.

For a moment, he seemed taken aback. Then, with a quizzical smile, he said, "Hi. It's nice to meet you."

At the sound of his voice, everything in Jill went still.

No! she thought wildly.

It couldn't be.

It simply *couldn't* be.

Afterward, she had no idea what she'd said at that point. She must have said hello. She must have smiled. She must have acted like an ordinary person. But at the time, she was in such a state of shock, she'd never be sure.

Elliott's brother.

The thought pounded through her.

Elliott's brother was the man she'd last seen almost eleven years ago. The man she'd known as Steve. The man she'd never, not in a million years, have imagined she'd ever see again.

The man who was Jordan's father.

Chapter Three

Stephen felt as if he'd been kicked in the stomach. When Elliott's fiancée had first walked into the room, Stephen had only thought how beautiful she was. It wasn't until Elliott brought her forward to introduce her, and Stephen had looked into her eyes, that he'd been shocked to realize she wasn't a stranger.

That in fact, the woman who had captured Elliott's heart was the girl he'd never been entirely able to forget.

J.J.

His J.J.

The beautiful nineteen-year-old with whom he'd spent five passion-filled days and nights at Padre Island during spring break when he was a twenty-two-year-old college senior.

He'd met her on the beach. She'd been with a group of girls; he'd been with some of his frat brothers. He still remembered the instant attraction that had ignited between them, an attraction that had only grown as the days went on. He also remembered how stung he'd been by the way she'd left without a word to him.

It had happened on Friday. They'd been together Thursday night, and after walking her back to her cottage at sunrise, they'd made arrangements to meet later that afternoon. But she hadn't shown up, and when he went to her cottage to see what had happened, one of her roommates said she'd been called home.

"Did she leave a message for me?" Stephen had asked.

The girl shook her head. "No, sorry."

Stephen almost asked if she knew J.J.'s home address or phone number, but something stopped him. Later, he wasn't sure if his hurt feelings had prevented him asking or if, on some level, he'd already known it was probably best to just forget about her.

After all, he was going back to Harvard and then would stay on for law school. And she was in college at Southwest Texas State University. Even that summer they would be thousands of miles apart, because he'd been offered a job as an aide in the Washington, D.C., office of a senator he greatly admired. And he knew she had a job lined up, too. So even though he'd felt regret, he'd told himself there was no point in trying to contact her again.

But he hadn't banked on just how hard it would be to forget her. Throughout the summer, at odd moments, she'd pop into his mind and stubbornly stay there. This happened most often when he was on a date. Somehow none of the girls he met that summer compared to J.J.

Many times over the years he'd wondered about

her. Wondered if she ever thought of him the way he thought of her.

But he'd never tried to find her. Hell, all they'd really had together was a one-week summer romance and some great sex. Nothing more. Maybe it could have developed into something else, but that time was long gone. He was resigned to never seeing her again.

But now here she was. In the flesh. And even more beautiful than she'd been as a girl.

His brother's bride-to-be.

Stephen's mind teemed with questions, yet how could he ask them? He knew she'd recognized him, too—he'd seen the knowledge in her eyes for one startled moment—but she hadn't acknowledged it, and under the circumstances, he didn't blame her. He doubted they would succeed in pretending they were simply casual acquaintances. He frantically searched his mind for something innocuous to say.

"Elliott tells me he met you in Austin?" he finally managed.

"Yes," she said faintly. Her face was pale.

"Like I told you, it was love at first sight," Elliott said, beaming. "At least, on my part."

Stephen hoped his smile disguised the turmoil going on inside of him. For the life of him, he couldn't think of a rejoinder.

"Well, *here* you all are."

All three turned at the sound of Caroline's voice.

"I didn't know you were having drinks," she continued with a frown.

"We've just started," Elliott said. "Join us. What would you like? And Jill? What can I get you?"

"Um, a glass of white wine?" Jill said.

"I want something stronger," Caroline said.

Although it was clear to Stephen that Caroline was not going to make much of an attempt to be pleasant, he welcomed her addition to the group. Knowing Caroline, she would dominate the conversation, taking the pressure off him.

Elliott walked over to the bar, and Caroline followed him. Jill, whose gaze flicked to Stephen, then quickly away, looked as if she wanted to be anywhere but there.

My God, she was beautiful with that cloud of golden-brown hair and those unbelievable tawny eyes with their thick eyelashes. Stephen couldn't take his eyes off of her. No wonder Elliott was so smitten. She still had that light dusting of freckles across her nose, he saw. He'd been entranced by those freckles.

Looking at her profile, he remembered how, after they'd made love, he would trace the lines of her face. Her skin had been incredibly soft and warm, and she'd always smelled like fresh flowers.

He swallowed. This situation was going to be impossible. How was he going to wipe those memories out of his mind when he was around her? How was he going to treat her the way he knew Elliott would want him to treat her?

"Here you go, darling," Elliott said, walking over and handing Jill her wine.

"Thank you." She smiled up at him.

Caroline rejoined them, a martini in hand. Eyes on Jill, she took a large swallow. "Are you feeling better now?" she asked.

"Thanks for asking, but I wasn't feeling bad. I guess I was just tired. I had a nap."

Caroline's expression was filled with disdain. "I don't believe in sleeping during the day."

Stephen looked at Elliott, whose own expression had hardened.

"Normally, I don't, either," Jill said pleasantly. "In fact, I couldn't believe how long I slept."

Before Caroline could answer, Tyler and another, smaller boy burst into the room.

"Mom, we're hungry!" Tyler said.

"You don't have to shout, Tyler," Caroline said, but there was no sting in her words. She adored and indulged her son who, in Stephen's opinion, was abominably spoiled.

"But we're *starving,* Mom," he said petulantly. "When're we gonna eat?"

Stephen looked curiously at the other boy, who hung back. He belatedly remembered that Caroline had told him Jill had a son. The boy was good-looking, with clear blue eyes and brownish-gold hair the same shade as his mother's. He smiled shyly when his gaze met Stephen's.

"Hi," Stephen said.

"Hi."

"This is Jordan, Jill's boy," Elliott said.

"It's nice to meet you," Stephen said. He stuck out his hand, and the boy took it. They shook gravely.

"Why don't you ask Marisol to give you a snack?" Elliott said to Tyler. "Tell her I said it was okay. Because it'll be another hour before dinner."

"Okay, Grandpa," Tyler said. "C'mon, Jordan. Let's go find Marisol."

Stephen noticed that Jordan looked to his mother before complying. When Jill nodded her okay, he took off after Tyler. Well behaved, then.

As the boys left the room, Stephen's gaze moved back to Jill. What was she thinking? he wondered, unable to fathom the expression in her eyes. Shaken, he looked away. Why hadn't he said something about knowing her? Now it was too late. Now if he said something, Elliott would wonder why he hadn't before.

And yet…

Stephen didn't like keeping something this important from Elliott. He had almost decided to try for a casual tone and say something like, *You know, Jill, you look familiar. Have we met before?*

But then Caroline said, "When did you meet Daddy?" Again the question was addressed to Jill.

By now Jill and Elliott were seated side by side on the large sofa that faced the fireplace, and Stephen had taken one of the side chairs. Caroline appropriated the rocking chair that had been her mother's favorite.

Smiling up at Elliott, Jill said, "Actually, we met because he came into the gallery where I worked to buy a birthday present for you, Caroline."

"This past birthday?" Caroline said sharply.

Stephen almost laughed at the myriad expressions that flitted across Caroline's face. He remembered how pleased she'd been with the painting. In fact, he'd heard her on the phone one day, bragging to one of her friends about the "good taste my father has." He could imagine what would happen to the painting now. It would probably soon adorn the nearest Dumpster.

"Jill's an art teacher *and* a wonderful artist," Elliott said. Once again, his voice rang with pride.

"So you just met in *February?*"

"Actually, it was in January," Elliott said.

Stephen wondered which was worse in Caroline's mind. The fact Elliott had only known Jill six months… or the fact that Adele had been dead only eight months when they'd met.

"The moment I set eyes on her I knew it was meant to be," Elliott said softly, turning his attention back to Jill.

Stephen couldn't look at Caroline. He knew exactly what she must be thinking now.

For a long moment, no one said anything. The grandfather clock, which had belonged to Elliott's paternal grandfather, chimed the hour. The chimes sounded ominous to Stephen.

He wished Caroline were different. Maybe if she were happy, she would be more inclined to want her father to be happy. Unfortunately, what happiness she did have seemed to be all wrapped up in filling her mother's role in Elliott's life. She reveled in playing hostess and in running his home. Now that role would be taken over by Jill.

He hoped Caroline would eventually come to terms with Elliott's coming marriage. That one of these days, she'd accept Jill, maybe even become friends with her.

But Stephen knew it was highly unlikely.

Poor Elliott. Whether he liked it or not, eventually he would have to choose between his daughter and Jill.

Realizing just what his brother had in store for him, Stephen knew he couldn't add to Elliott's worries or give Caroline any more ammunition to use against Jill. Best to keep pretending this was the first time he'd ever seen her.

Decision made, he tried to relax. When Marisol finally announced dinner, Stephen rose gratefully. Just another hour or so, and he could escape to his own home.

He tried not to think about the future.

And he dared not think about the past.

Jill couldn't wait for dinner to be over. She was so nervous, she could hardly eat.

"Aren't you feeling well, darling?" Elliott finally asked her, brows knitting in concern.

"I— My stomach's a little upset." Jill had a hard time meeting his eyes. This was the first time she'd ever lied to Elliott, and she didn't like the feeling.

Why had this happened? Why, of all the millions of people in Texas, had she had to meet and become engaged to the brother of her son's father? Was God trying to play a joke on her?

She kept telling herself she had nothing to worry about. Stephen didn't know he was Jordan's father. No one knew except her. She'd never even told her aunt, saying only that she'd met a boy on spring break. Her Aunt Harriett—who was as old-fashioned as they come—had been very disappointed in Jill, but she loved her, and she'd encouraged her to have her baby and keep it. When Jordan was born, she'd loved him, too, and she'd been thrilled when Jill had given him her surname. Unfortunately, she hadn't had a long time to enjoy him since her second heart attack when he was three proved to be fatal.

Jill still missed her. She had been a wonderful person. She was Jill's mother Hannah's twin, and when Harriett died it was like losing her mother all over again.

Jill took a sip of her wine. She had been avoiding looking at Stephen, who sat across the table from her, but now she sneaked a glance at him. Her heart lurched when her gaze connected with his, and she looked away.

Steve. Elliott's Stephen is my Steve. Jordan's father! This is impossible. I can't live here.

And yet, what could she do?

This was Elliott's home. He would never leave the ranch. It was in his blood; he loved it. And she was soon to be Elliott's wife.

Jill's stomach roiled. She knew she could not continue to sit there acting as if everything was wonderful. Leaning toward Elliott, she said quietly, "I'm feeling worse, Elliott. Do you mind if—?"

"Of course not, darling," he said, not even letting her finish. "Ask Marisol to give you an antacid or something and then why don't you go back to the guesthouse?" He squeezed her hand. "I'll come by and say good night before I turn in."

Jill felt like a worm. Lower than a worm. He was such a good man. What would he think if he knew what had upset her? What would any of them think?

Oh, God, if Caroline should ever find out! She detests me now. If she knew the truth, my days here would definitely be numbered.

"Mom?" Jordan said. "Are you okay?"

Guiltily, Jill looked at her son. "Yes, honey. I—I just need something to settle my stomach. You finish your dinner, then come see me, all right?" She forced a smile. "I'll tuck you in."

Jordan nodded. His eyes were worried.

Jill knew why. She was never sick. And Jordan was

protective of her. They'd been each other's only family for a long time. "Finish your dinner, okay?" she added in a lighter tone.

"Okay."

"I'll walk him over later," Elliott said. "Don't worry."

"Good night, everyone," Jill said. "Sorry to be such a wet blanket." As she walked out of the room into the foyer, she knew they were all watching her.

When she shut the door of the guesthouse behind her, she sagged in relief, leaning against it and closing her eyes. She was shaking from the release of tension. And yet, this was only a temporary reprieve. What about tomorrow night? And all the nights to come?

Could she do this?

Could she marry Elliott? Build a good life with him in spite of Stephen's presence here?

But what was the alternative? She'd already quit her job. Her furniture and belongings were in storage and would soon be on their way to the ranch. And her little house, the first she'd ever bought, was already on the market.

But those things were the least of it. If she didn't go through with her marriage to Elliott, she would hurt him terribly. And Jordan. She would hurt him, too, because he was overjoyed at the turn of events. He loved Elliott.

Maybe she should just come clean. Tell Elliott everything. But how could she? If all there was to confess was her prior relationship with Stephen, she might have been able to do it. But there was Jordan to consider. And even if she *didn't* tell Elliott about Stephen's relationship to Jordan, wouldn't Elliott eventually figure it out? Surely he would ask questions. Think about the dates involved.

Put two and two together. Then what? Would he even *want* to marry her when he knew the whole truth?

Dear God. What am I going to do?

I have no good choices.

"Nora?"

"Jill? What a nice surprise! I didn't expect to hear from you so soon."

It was the next morning. Elliott had gotten up early and was out on the ranch somewhere. Before he'd left, he'd put a note under her door saying he was taking Jordan with him and that they'd be back before lunch. Jill had eaten her breakfast alone in the main house because no one except Marisol was around. Afterward, she'd carried a steaming mug of coffee back to the guesthouse, shut the door and taken advantage of her solitude to call Nora.

"So tell me *everything!*" Nora said.

"Oh, God, Nora, I wish you were here."

"What's the matter, honey? You sound upset."

Jill swallowed. Hearing Nora's voice had brought everything to the fore. Made her realize just how serious, how truly impossible, her situation was. "I desperately need someone to talk to," she finally said. She had tried to keep her voice level and calm, but she heard the shaky note.

"Jill?" Nora said softly. "What *is* it?"

Tears pooled in Jill's yes. "I—I can't talk about it on the phone. I'm not sure I should talk about it at all. I—I've never told anyone."

There was silence for a long moment. "This has to do with Jordan's father, doesn't it?"

Jill nodded. Then, realizing Nora couldn't see her, whispered, "Yes."

"Has he somehow contacted you…or something?"

Jill knew Nora had often wondered about Jordan's father. Once, they'd spoken of it, and Jill had admitted that he was someone she'd met on spring break at Padre Island when she was only nineteen and she'd never seen him since. "He never knew about my pregnancy," she'd confessed. She'd never told Nora his name or anything about him. Now she took a deep breath and said, "He's here."

"*There?* You mean in High Creek?"

"Worse. He's here at the ranch."

"He *works* there? Good Lord."

"Oh, Nora. H-he's Elliott's brother."

"Elliott's brother!"

"Well, his *half* brother."

After a stunned silence of several seconds, Nora said, "Did you know about him?"

"I knew Elliott had a half brother. And I knew his name was Stephen, but that's all I knew. I never, in a million years, associated him with…with Jordan's father. The truth is, I knew Steve's—I called him Steve, not Stephen—last name was Wells, but Elliott never referred to his brother by his last name. All he ever said was Stephen, and I never asked. It didn't seem important. In fact, I never even thought about asking." Only now did she remember that Elliott had mentioned his brother was a lawyer, but there were thousands of lawyers, maybe even millions of lawyers.

"Oh, Jill. Does…does he know?"

"You mean Stephen?"

"Yes."

"About Jordan?"

"Yes."

"Well, he met Jordan, of course. But know he's *his* son? No, of course not."

"But he recognized *you?*"

Jill thought about the look on Stephen's face when realization dawned. "Yes, he recognized me, just as I recognized him."

"Oh, my God," Nora said. "What are you going to do?"

Again, Jill's eyes filled with tears, and she angrily brushed them away. Tears were worthless. Right now what she needed was strength and straight thinking. "I don't know. At dinner last night my head was spinning."

"I take it he…this Stephen…didn't acknowledge that he knew you."

"No. And I didn't, either. I mean, it was such a shock, and I couldn't think. And then, when I could, it was too late. Even if I'd wanted to say, 'Aren't you the boy I met years ago at Padre Island,' I couldn't. It would seem strange that I hadn't said something immediately. Besides, then I would have had to lie, because I certainly couldn't have admitted that Steve— Stephen—was someone I'd had a passionate affair with." Oh, God. Did he remember those nights as vividly as she did?

"And I'm sure he felt the same way," Nora said reflectively. "I mean, I'm assuming he cares about Elliott."

"They're very close. Elliott admitted to me once that he's closer to Stephen than he is to his daughter, that he loves him like a son, and I think Stephen feels the same way."

"Good Lord," Nora said. "What a mess." After a

moment, she added, "I wish I was there. Not that I could do anything, but I could lend moral support."

"You don't know how much I wish you were here, too."

Nora was a bit older, in her early forties, divorced and childless. She was one of the most centered, stable people Jill had ever known, with a dry wit and the ability to laugh at herself—a trait Jill admired almost more than anything else. People who took themselves too seriously were deadly bores, she felt.

"Hey, do you *want* me to come? I'm due for some vacation. And Brian could oversee the gallery for a couple of days…or even a week."

"Oh, Nora, that would be wonderful. Would you?"

"Would Elliott mind?"

Jill smiled. "Elliott will love that you're coming." She didn't add that Elliott would love anything that made her happy. She didn't have to. Wasn't Nora the one who had urged her to marry Elliott?

"So what about the daughter?"

"Why don't I just wait and let you see for yourself what she's like?"

"That bad, huh?" Nora said wryly.

Jill grimaced. "I shouldn't judge her after just one day."

"Hey, I can usually size someone up after just one hour, and you're no slouch in that department, either."

"Maybe, in this case, I'm too prejudiced to be fair. After all, to her, I'm an interloper here, and I'm younger than she is. If I were in her shoes, I'd probably hate me, too. But let's not talk about her now. I want you to meet her first, give her a chance to settle down a bit. So," she said more brightly, "when can you be here?"

"How long a drive is it?"

"It took us about five hours."

"Let's say tomorrow afternoon, then. If there's a problem with Brian, I'll call you back."

"Oh, Nora, thank you. Elliott told me he's invited a few close friends to come and meet me Saturday night. I was a bit nervous about it even before I knew about Stephen, so I'm really glad you'll be here, too."

After Jill gave Nora directions, she said goodbye. Once the connection was broken, Jill sat there thinking. Knowing Nora was coming made Jill feel better. Maybe she was being too dramatic about everything, making a mountain out of a molehill. Maybe there was some reasonable solution to her problem, something she couldn't see, but Nora would.

At the very least, with Nora there, Jill would feel less alone.

Chapter Four

"I'm so glad you're here," Jill said for perhaps the hundredth time since Nora had arrived.

The two women were dressing for the evening in Jill's bedroom. Although Elliott had objected, saying they'd be more comfortable if Nora took one of the guest bedrooms in the main house, Jill had insisted upon giving her bedroom to Nora, and Jill herself would sleep in the other twin bed in Jordan's room for the duration of Nora's visit.

"I don't mind at all," she'd told Elliott. "It'll be fun. We'll probably be staying up till all hours talking."

Sleeping arrangements at the ranch were delicate, anyway. Jill knew Caroline was probably convinced that when Nora wasn't around Elliott would probably sneak out at night and join Jill in her bedroom. Stephen probably thought so, too.

The truth was, Jill had made it clear to Elliott up front how she felt. And he had completely understood her belief that an intimate relationship between them would be a very bad example to set for Jordan. "We can only be together if Jordan spends the night somewhere else," she'd explained.

It was Elliott who made the decision that he could wait until they were married. "It won't be easy," he'd said. "But you're worth it."

"You look awfully serious," Nora said.

"Oh, sorry." Jill wished she could stop thinking about her problems. This was supposed to be a happy time for her—the beginning of a new chapter in her life. "I was daydreaming, I guess."

"Worrying is more like it."

Jill made a face. "You know me too well." She fluffed her hair, wishing she'd had time to get it trimmed before leaving Austin.

"You look wonderful," Nora said.

Jill studied herself in the full-length cheval mirror. Tonight she wore brown linen slacks and a coral sleeveless sweater. "Do you think so?" she asked doubtfully. "I'm not sure about this sweater."

"It's beautiful. What's your problem?"

Nora herself wore black linen pants, a matching tunic top and chunky silver jewelry. As always, she looked sophisticated and classy.

"I wish I could wear black," Jill said. She leaned closer to the mirror and inspected her face. Was that a pimple on her chin?

"Black isn't your thing," Nora said. "You look great. Stop stalling."

"I'm not stalling. I think I have a pimple."

"Oh, for heaven's sake. Your skin is perfect. And you are, too, stalling. I, on the other hand, can hardly wait."

Nora had arrived at the ranch a couple of hours earlier. She had yet to meet Caroline or Stephen and she was unabashedly impatient.

The words were barely out of her mouth when there was a knock at Jill's bedroom door followed by "Mom! I'm goin' over to the house."

"Jordan, wait for us." She walked over and opened the door. "I just have to put on my jewelry and we'll be ready to go."

Jordan, who had spent the entire day outside with Elliott, had showered earlier and was now dressed in clean jeans and a yellow shirt. His first choice had been a much-beloved Brad Paisley T-shirt paired with ragged jeans, but Jill had quickly squashed that idea.

"Well, hurry up," her son said now.

She couldn't help laughing. "If you stop whining, I will."

He rolled his eyes and plopped down on her bed. His expression said grown-ups were weird.

Jill reached for her jewelry. Diamond stud earrings— a gift from Elliott in April on her birthday, a thin, silver bangle bracelet and her diamond engagement ring completed Jill's preparations.

The ring had been a bone of contention between her and Elliott. She felt it was much too big—a two-carat, round diamond set in platinum. Jill could only imagine how much it had cost. But Elliott wouldn't listen, saying he couldn't take the ring back and that he wanted her to have it, period. Jill had reluctantly given in, although she had to admit the ring was gorgeous. She was probably the only woman on earth who would rather have something smaller and simpler.

After one last glance in the mirror, she sighed and said, "Let's go."

Ten minutes later, the three of them walked into the main house, and Jill—who had a stomach full of butterflies—told herself to settle down.

Earlier she had decided tonight was a test. If she could behave normally, if she could survive the entire evening in both Stephen's and Caroline's company without giving anything of her feelings away, then maybe everything would work out here. Maybe she really *could* marry Elliott and make a good life with him.

Please, God, she prayed as they walked into the living room. *Help me.*

Stephen would have known Jill had entered the room even if he hadn't been watching for her, because the atmosphere immediately changed.

His mouth went dry at the sight of her. What was it about this woman that had the power to affect him so strongly? Sure, she was beautiful, but he'd known lots of beautiful women. Hell, Emily was just as beautiful. Maybe even more so, with her white-blond hair and dancer's body. *Damn.* Emily. What was he going to do about her?

Most people in High Creek assumed the two of them would get married. Stephen knew Elliott hoped so, for he had made no secret of how much he liked Emily. But tonight, watching Jill, feeling what he was feeling, Stephen knew why he hadn't committed wholeheartedly to Emily before now. It was because he'd never felt toward her what he felt toward Jill. Jill, who was completely off-limits. Jill, a woman he shouldn't even think about, let alone covet. *Your brother's fiancée. Don't ever forget it.* He swallowed. *I'm in such big trouble.*

"Jill, darling, there you are," said Elliott, moving forward to meet her and her friend.

Stephen reluctantly tore his gaze away from Jill and trained it on the woman who had entered the room with her. Tall, attractive, with short black hair and large, curious eyes, she seemed perfectly at ease, even though normally well-mannered Elliott—obsessed with Jill—seemed to have forgotten she was there.

Stephen walked over to her. "Hi. I'm Stephen, Elliott's brother."

She smiled. "Nora O'Malley." She offered her hand.

Her handshake was firm, no nonsense. Her brown eyes met his directly. "It's nice to meet you."

Funny how you could meet a person and immediately know you'd like them. Stephen sensed this was a woman you could depend upon and trust. Yet there was also something about her gaze that made him slightly uneasy. He doubted you could fool this woman.

"Can I get you a drink?" he offered.

"Thank you. I'd love a glass of white wine."

"Chardonnay? Pinot grigio? Riesling?"

"Pinot grigio would be great."

Stephen walked to the bar, uncorked a bottle, poured her the wine, then carried it back to where she stood. While he'd been gone, she'd been joined by Jill and Elliott. Stephen couldn't help it; his heartbeat accelerated. He mentally grimaced. What the hell was wrong with him? He was a grown-up. He should be able to control his impulses. Instead he was behaving like a hormonal kid.

"Here you go." He handed the wineglass to Nora. Was he imagining it, or was there a glint of amusement in her eyes? His own gaze moved involuntarily to Jill and Elliott.

"I'm not being a very good host," Elliott said. He turned to Nora. "I see you've met Stephen. And here comes my daughter." Motioning for Caroline, who— along with Tyler—had just entered the room, to join them, he added, "Caroline, this is Nora O'Malley, the friend of Jill's I was telling you about earlier."

Stephen was relieved to see that Caroline was on her best behavior tonight. She walked forward, shook Nora's hand, said she was pleased to meet her, even smiled and said she'd heard about her gallery.

"I go to Austin fairly often. That's where I went to school, and I still have friends there," Caroline said. "I'll have to come by the next time I'm in town."

"I'd like that," Nora said.

"I understand you handle a lot of Jill's paintings."

"I do."

"I'll look forward to seeing them."

What was going on? Stephen wondered. Had Caroline had a change of heart? He found that hard to believe. She must have some kind of ulterior motive for her sudden agreeableness, but what it was, he couldn't fathom. Had his brother talked to her? He looked at Elliott, who kept a possessive arm around Jill and beamed happily. Was it Stephen's imagination, or did Jill look uncomfortable? For a moment, their eyes met, but she quickly looked away.

Unbidden, a memory surfaced. It had been late one night. The beach had been deserted. Most of the kids had either headed for bed or one of the local hangouts. Under a full moon, Stephen and J.J. slow danced on the sand. Stephen remembered vividly what her body had felt like moving against his. How much he'd wanted her, even though they had already made love twice that night.

He gulped. Tried to push the memory away. But it refused to go. And his traitorous body responded to it. He knew he had to get away, get himself under control.

Spying the boys, who were attacking the cheese dip and tortilla chips Marisol had put out earlier, Stephen excused himself and walked over to them on the pretense of wanting something to eat himself.

"So what do you think of the ranch?" he said to Jordan.

The boy grinned. "It's great! I hope we stay here forever. Elliott let me ride Gypsy today. Do you know Gypsy?" At Stephen's amused nod, he said, "Boy, she's a cool horse. And Elliott said when I learn to ride better, he'll get me a horse of my own!"

Stephen couldn't help laughing at the boy's enthusiasm. "She *is* a great horse. We've had her a long time." Gypsy was the gentlest, sweetest-natured mare in their stables—there for the express purpose of allowing visiting greenhorns to ride and feel a part of things.

"Elliott said I'm gonna be sore tomorrow," Jordan said. His mouth was full of chips.

Stephen nodded and tried not to grin. Boys never changed. "Riding's hard on the backside."

Tyler made a face. "I hate riding."

Jordan gave Tyler a stunned look. "You *do?*"

"Yeah. It sucks."

Stephen knew why his nephew felt the way he did. Tyler was one of the most non-athletic kids Stephen had ever known. Unfortunately, in this area his mother wouldn't cut him any slack. Caroline was an expert horsewoman; she'd won dozens of medals throughout her adolescence, and she expected no less from her son. That Tyler had other talents didn't matter. The fact that he was a math whiz and that his guitar teacher thought he could have a career in music if he really wanted it wasn't enough for her; she expected her son to excel at sports, too.

Maybe I should talk to Dale again. Stephen had remained friends with Caroline's ex after the divorce, which was just one more black mark against him in Caroline's book. Trouble with talking to Dale, though, was the fact that he couldn't do much to change things as far as Tyler was concerned. No matter what Dale might suggest or try to implement concerning his son, Caroline would undermine it, just on general principles.

"Uncle Stephen?"

Stephen turned his attention back to the boys.

"Will you take me and Jordan flying?"

Both Tyler and Jordan looked at him eagerly.

"If your mothers say it's okay, sure. If the weather's good, maybe we could go on Sunday." He was rewarded with big smiles. Funny how much nicer Tyler could be when his mother's attention was somewhere else. He began to animatedly describe to Jordan what it was like to go up in Stephen's plane.

Although Stephen was ostensibly talking to the boys, he had kept one ear tuned to the conversation behind him. Caroline still sounded pleasant, and there was quite a bit of laughter. He wondered if Jill was as unnerved by the situation as he was, but better able to disguise it. Stephen couldn't get the unbelievable situation out of his mind. All night last night he'd thought about the unlikely turn of events and tried to figure out what to do. He knew he was going to have to talk to Jill. To others they might have to keep pretending they didn't know each other, but eventually the truth would have to be faced between them. How could it not? As far as he was concerned, that truth was like the elephant in the room. Impossible to ignore.

Somehow he had to find a way to talk to her in private. In fact, after his two scheduled appointments that morning—one involving a change to a will and the other an interview with a potential witness in a custody suit—he had come out to the ranch to see if he might be able to get her alone, but she wasn't in the main house and he couldn't think of any plausible reason to seek her out in the guesthouse.

He'd left in frustration, wondering if there might be a way to phone her and ask her to meet with him in town. He was sure she probably had a cell phone, but how could he get the number without raising suspicion?

These questions continued to plague him until Marisol announced dinner. And even though he tried to banish them and simply concentrate on acting as normal as possible throughout the rest of the evening, they refused to leave him alone.

Because the bottom line was, he had a decision to make. And until he talked to Jill, he wouldn't be able to make it.

Jill knew one thing for sure. If Stephen were still living at the ranch, even if he ate all his *meals* at the ranch, she wouldn't have been able to stay. It would have been unbearable for her to constantly be in his company. As it was, he came much too often. Elliott had said that Stephen gave him two, sometimes three days a week.

"He spends Mondays, Wednesdays and Fridays in town at his law office," he'd explained. "And the rest of the time, he tends to ranch business." Elliott had smiled. "But that's not set in stone. If I need him more often, he changes his schedule. After all, the ranch is half his. I told you, didn't I, that it belonged to our mother's family? In fact, until her father, my Granddad Tyler, died, it was even called The Tyler Ranch. Some folks around here still refer to it that way."

Jill had nodded. But all she could think about, then and now, was that Stephen would *always* be there. Jill already felt as if she was in a permanent state of anxiety, never sure when she would see him, never able to really relax, and she'd only been here a couple of days. How was she going to live the rest of her life this way?

And yet…she couldn't deny that a part of her wanted to see him. See him and talk about him.

"So what did you think of Stephen?" she asked Nora. It was the following morning and the two women were getting ready to go over to the main house for breakfast.

"I liked him." Nora had just gotten out of the shower and she was towel drying her hair. "He's a lot like Elliott, you know." Her gaze was thoughtful. "In fact, that might have something to do with why you were drawn to Elliott in the first place."

Jill sat on the bed. Could Nora be right? Had her subconscious been at work? She shrugged. "Maybe."

Nora finished drying her hair and rummaged in her

overnight case, eventually pulling out a comb. "He couldn't keep his eyes off you last night, especially during dinner. He kept trying not to look at you, but he lost the battle."

"Really?"

"Really."

"Well, if that's true, it's not a good thing. I can just imagine what he was thinking."

"You didn't see the expression in his eyes," Nora said. She'd finished with her hair and sat down next to Jill.

"I'm sure he thinks I'm a terrible person." Did he?

"Why would he think that? He's just as much at fault for this situation you're in as you are."

"What if he thinks I got engaged to Elliott on purpose? Maybe he thinks I knew the whole time that Elliott was his brother and this is just some kind of ploy to be near Stephen."

"Oh, Jill, for heaven's sake. Of course he doesn't think that. Didn't you tell me that during the time you spent together years ago the two of you said very little about your families? Did you, for instance, tell him your aunt's name? Or where she lived?"

"Other than in San Marcos, you mean?"

"Yes."

Jill thought back. Had she? She didn't remember doing so. The truth was, the whole time she and Stephen were together, they mostly spent having sex. Thrilling, wonderful, exciting sex. "I'm sure I referred to her as my Aunt Harriett, but I don't think I said much else. He…wouldn't have known her last name because it was Jordan, not Emerson."

"I rest my case," Nora said, getting up. "Now I'm

going to go put on my makeup so we can go, because I'm hungry."

"Wait, Nora. Let's not go yet. We won't be able to talk over at the main house. Caroline might be there and Marisol will definitely be there."

"Speaking of Caroline, has the woman ever had a *job?* I'd think she'd go nuts out here living off her father."

"She's not living off Elliott. She has her own trust fund. Part of it came from her mother, the rest of it comes from the ranch itself. Plus, she gets child support from her ex. So whether she lives here or not, she doesn't have any financial worries." Elliott had explained all this to Jill because he hadn't wanted her to feel guilty or worry that their marriage would affect Caroline financially.

Nora snorted. "Do her good to work for a living, I would think. Her problem is she's been Daddy's princess all her life, but you know what? It's time for Miss Caroline to grow up."

"I know, and you're right, but I don't want to talk about Caroline right now. I have a more pressing problem and need to make a decision. Do you think I should tell Elliott the truth about Stephen?"

"Hon, I already told you…this is something only you can decide."

"But you think I should, I know you do."

Nora sighed and sat down again. "All right. Knowing you and what a straight arrow you are, I don't believe you'll be able to live a lie. I think the stress will eventually do you in."

Jill nodded miserably. That's what she thought, too. Yet knowing what she should do and having the courage to actually do it were two different things.

"If it were just me who would be affected—if Jordan didn't exist—then there'd be no question in my mind," she said slowly. "Of course, I'd tell him. But Jordan *does* exist. And any decision I make affects him just as much as it affects me…maybe even more." She swallowed. "He wants a father so badly and he's already so attached to Elliott…"

"I know," Nora said, putting her arm around Jill.

Jill bit her lip. Why? Why had this happened? They'd only been here at the ranch for a few days, and her son was already happier than she'd ever seen him. How could she take that away from him? Because Jill was certain that once she told Elliott the truth, he would no longer want to marry her.

"What about Stephen?"

"What about him?"

"How do you feel about him now that you've seen him again?"

Jill couldn't meet Nora's eyes. "I—I don't know." But even as she said the words, she knew they were a lie. And when she finally did look at Nora, she could tell Nora knew they were a lie, too.

"If Elliott wasn't a factor," Nora prompted in her relentless way, "what then?"

"But Elliott *is* a factor."

"You're skirting the question."

"I'm not. I… Oh, God, Elliott's been so good to me."

"Admit it. You still have feelings for Stephen."

Jill's eyes filled with tears. "God help me," she whispered.

"Do you want him to be a part of Jordan's life?"

"How *can* he be?"

Nora chuckled. "I know this is a serious situation, but Jill, honey, you're talking like a politician, answering every question with a question."

Right then Jill was too miserable to laugh at herself. After a long moment, she said, "You're the only person in the world I could say this to, but yes, in an ideal world, I'd tell Stephen the truth and pray that he'd want to be a part of Jordan's life."

"And what about *your* life?"

But Jill couldn't answer that question. She couldn't because she was afraid to.

Chapter Five

"How do the boots fit?" Jill asked. She and Nora had gone to town that morning to buy boots for Nora because Elliott was taking them on a tour of the ranch—including the stables—today, and Nora wanted to ride.

"Great. I love them!" Nora stuck her right foot out, twisting it this way and that, to admire the distressed leather cowgirl boots they'd found on sale at the local Western store. "Now that I look the part, maybe I'll take up country-and-western dancing."

Jill laughed. She wore sturdy leather boots that she'd bought in Austin. She'd actually been on a horse before; Nora hadn't, so this afternoon would be interesting.

True to his promise, instead of eating with the workers, as he did most days, Elliott joined Jill and Nora for lunch. Afterward, the two women piled into his

Jeep Wrangler and they were off. "I'll take you on a general tour of the ranch first, then we'll circle back to where we stable and work with the horses," Elliott said.

Jordan was already down at the stables, where he now seemed to spend most of the daylight hours. Antonio, the barn manager and Marisol's husband, had taken Jordan under his wing. Antonio was responsible for hiring and supervising all the "boys" who cleaned out stalls, groomed, fed and watered the horses, walked them to and from the pastures, and cooled them down after exercise. Jordan tagged along after Antonio like his shadow.

"I'm helping him, Mom," Jordan said indignantly when she'd said she hoped he wasn't being a nuisance. "He's teaching me how to do stuff." Elliott had reassured her that Antonio, a doting grandfather himself, enjoyed having Jordan around.

Thinking about Jordan and how happy he seemed, Jill couldn't help but smile.

As they bumped along the unpaved road leading toward the northwest part of the ranch, Elliott kept up a running commentary about the terrain and ranching, mostly for Nora's benefit. Jill had heard most of this before, but she still found it fascinating. She'd never imagined she would live on a ranch, let alone be married to a wealthy rancher. Her life had been spent in urban areas; she was a city girl through and through, yet the romantic lore of cowboys and ranching had captured her imagination.

"How big *is* the ranch?" Nora asked.

"Thirty-two thousand acres," Elliott said.

"How many miles is that?"

"Fifty square miles," Jill answered proudly. When Elliott gave her a surprised look, she laughed. "I looked it up."

"That's my girl."

About fifteen minutes later, the road climbed to a rise and when they reached its peak, Elliott stopped. From their vantage point, they could see dozens of oil derricks spread out below, as well as several buildings. Three or four men also were visible.

"We can go closer, if you like," Elliott said as they climbed out of the truck. "But this is the best view of the operation."

"What do those men down there do?" Nora asked.

"That depends," Elliott said. "Some are mechanics or safety inspectors. Others might be engineers, and from time to time there's a geologist or two on site."

Nora shaded her eyes as she studied the scene. Although all three of them wore sunglasses today, the sun was blinding. "So you don't really have anything to do with the day-to-day operation?"

Elliott shook his head. "I don't have anything to do with the operation, period. All I do is collect checks four times a year." He grimaced. "We have an agreement with an oil company. They lease the land, pay all the expenses of testing, drilling and bringing up the oil, and our family gets a percentage of what they find."

"You don't seem that happy about it."

"I know I should be grateful," Elliott said, "but the truth is, I miss the old days, before oil was discovered, when we were a real working ranch. 'Course, half the time we were struggling to make ends meet. Now there's plenty of money for our horse breeding operation." He made a face. "Trouble is, like most people, I want to have my cake and eat it, too."

Jill reached over and squeezed his hand. She knew he was constantly torn by his conflicting feelings.

Join the club, she thought wryly. Lately all she did was think about her own conflicting feelings. Resolutely, she pushed the thought away. She'd promised herself that today belonged to Elliott, that she absolutely would not think about Stephen.

"Where's the boundary of your land?" Nora asked.

"See that thicket of trees over there?" Elliott pointed north. "That fence behind it? That's the boundary between us and the Vincenti spread. The Vincenti family is the reason we got into the oil business to begin with. Oil was discovered on their land first. After that, we were approached by the same oil company." Turning to Jill, he added, "You'll meet Pete Saturday night. He's one of my oldest friends."

They watched a few minutes longer, then got into the Jeep and headed back the way they'd come. Awhile later, about half a mile before reaching the main house, the road they were on branched off to the west and soon multiple buildings, an outdoor riding arena and nearby pastures came into view.

As they got closer, Jill could see that the area was a beehive of activity. Elliott pulled into a large black-topped parking area. The main barn rose up two stories and rather than typical red planking, it was a pale cream with hunter green window frames hung with flower boxes. The structure looked more like a light industrial park than a place for livestock. There were half a dozen other vehicles parked in the vicinity, mostly dusty pickup trucks, but several luxury SUVs, as well.

"We'll start with the stables and tack room," Elliott said, leading the way.

Jill took off her sunglasses when they entered the barn. She had expected a typical barnlike mustiness; she was pleasantly surprised. Instead as soon as she walked down the cleanly swept aisle, her impression was new leather, fresh wood shavings and cut hay. The smell of horse—not unpleasant—permeated everything.

Her first impression was one of organized bustle: a man grooming a horse in cross-ties in a grooming stall, another inspecting a horse's ears, another cleaning a horse's hoof with a hoof pick, two men conferring at the other end of the stable area, another barking orders on a cell phone. There were twelve enormous box stalls, six on each side facing each other across a wide aisle hung with halters and lead lines.

About midway through the main area, she saw Jordan standing on an upturned bucket and leaning over the gate to one of the stalls. He was stroking the nose of the horse inside. There was a man standing beside him, and at first Jill thought it was Antonio, but then the man turned.

It was Stephen.

Jill's heart seized. Somehow, seeing father and son together like this hit her hard. Dear heaven, they were so alike. She couldn't believe that no one else could see what she saw. Tears clogged her throat, and she wasn't sure she would be able to speak. Dazed, she stumbled. Elliott, who was in front of her, didn't see and kept walking, but Nora grabbed her.

"What is it?" she said in alarm.

"I—I can't… I have to get out of here."

"Jill," Nora whispered urgently, "snap out of it. Stephen's watching you. Do you want him to know how he affects you?"

Jill took a shuddering breath. Swallowed. "No."

"Then plaster a smile on your face. And let's go."

It was one of the hardest things she'd ever done, but Jill managed to follow Nora's orders.

"Mom!" Jordan called out when he spied her. "This is Gypsy! I told you about her. She's the horse I ride. Isn't she the *best?*"

"She certainly is." The mare was beautiful, with soft brown eyes, a shining russet coat, and a gentle look about her.

Jordan was obviously beside himself with happiness, for his face and eyes glowed. "Stephen's been telling me all about Gypsy and the babies she's had. One of 'em is over there!" Jordan pointed to a stall across the way. "His name is Big Boy. Isn't that a cool name? He belongs to Stephen and Stephen said when I get more experience, maybe I can ride him. Wouldn't that be great?"

Jill had herself under control now—Jordan's excitement had helped—and she smiled, first at her son, then at Elliott, and finally, at Stephen. "Looks like you've made Jordan's day."

"My pleasure," Stephen said. He ruffled Jordan's hair. "This young man is going to be an excellent horseman."

Jordan beamed.

Just then, Antonio called from the other end of the stable area. "Mr. Lawrence! Can you come here for a minute? I've got Walter Zewickly on the phone."

"I'll be right back," Elliott said.

"So tell me about Gypsy," Nora said to Jordan.

Jordan eagerly complied and Jill pretended to be interested, but she was all too aware of Stephen standing there watching her, because he made no secret of it. Unable to stop herself, her eyes met his. The moment they did, he inclined his head in a way that clearly said he wanted to talk to her, but not right there.

Her heart galloped as she followed him over to Big Boy's stall. As soon as they were out of earshot of the others, he said, "We have to talk. Can you come into town on Monday?"

"I—I guess so." *Dear heaven.*

"Do you have a cell phone?"

"Yes."

"Give me the number. I'll call you Monday morning." He repeated the number twice, then said he'd remember it. Then, louder, he said, "He's a beauty, isn't he?" He stroked the gelding's head. "I promise I won't let Jordan ride him until I'm sure he's ready."

A second later, Elliott joined them. He was smiling.

"What did Walt have to say?" Stephen asked. "Is he in?"

"Yep. He's in." When Elliott began to give Stephen details of his phone call, Jill walked back over to Nora and Jordan.

Nora looked at her.

"I'll tell you later," Jill said. Her mind was spinning. Today was only Thursday. She'd have to wait four days to find out what Stephen wanted. Four days of agonizing and worrying.

How could she stand it?

Yet what choice did she have?

* * *

"Knock, knock."

Stephen's head jerked up. He'd been so engrossed in the contract he was working on, he hadn't heard Emily's approach, but there she was, in his open doorway, a big smile on her face. As always, she was a showstopper, the kind of woman who drew admiring glances wherever she went. Today her thick, white-blond hair was in her workaday mode—caught up in a high ponytail, then twisted around to form a tight bun. A form-fitting white tank top paired with a flowing red print skirt and red ballet flats completed her ensemble.

All were set off by her tanned skin. She'd once told him she knew it wasn't healthy to love the sun as she did, but growing up in Sweden and being deprived of sun for so many months during the year, she just couldn't resist it. Otherwise very sensible, on this one point she seemed unable to change.

"Welcome back," he said, wishing he were happier to see her. "You're home early."

Still smiling, she walked into the office. "Yes. I got in last night."

"Good trip?"

"Wonderful." She walked around to the back of his desk and leaned over to give him a kiss.

"How's your dad doing?" One of the reasons Emily had gone to Sweden earlier this year—she usually visited in July when the weather was warmest—was because her father had had a stroke.

"He's doing really well. His doctors think he'll fully recover. Apparently it was a very mild stroke." She pushed some papers out of the way and sat on the edge of his desk.

"That's good. I know how worried you were." He tried not to be irritated at her proprietary air.

"Of course. He's only fifty-six, and we Swedes expect to live a lot longer than that."

Stephen nodded. Fifty-six was young. Hell, Elliott was fifty-seven, and Stephen never thought of him as old.

"Um, is this a bad time?" she asked, apparently sensing his irritation.

Stephen immediately felt like a jerk. It wasn't *her* fault he had such conflicted feelings about her. "I'm never too busy to spend a few minutes talking to you. Have a seat. I'll ask Sandra to bring us something to drink."

"Don't bother Sandra. I was actually hoping you'd join me for lunch." Instead of moving to sit in one of the two chairs flanking his desk, she remained perched on the edge of his desk. "I was thinking Lou's for hamburgers."

"Em, I can't, not today. I've got a contract to finish writing before my two o'clock appointment and it's going to be a tight squeeze as it is."

Disappointment immediately clouded her green eyes. "But you have to eat."

"Sandra'll go out and get me a sub or something. I planned to just eat here at my desk." He felt bad seeing how she tried to mask the disappointment. He almost changed his mind. The world wouldn't end if he didn't finish the contract this morning. After all, it had nothing to do with his two o'clock appointment, which he knew he'd led her to believe.

Christ, what was wrong with him? Most men would kill to have a woman like Emily. She had everything: she was beautiful, talented, sexy, nice. But as much as he liked her and enjoyed her company—and, if he was being completely honest, the sex—he wasn't in love with her, a fact he'd finally faced. The reason he'd finally faced it wasn't something he cared to examine too closely.

Looking at her now, seeing the hurt she was trying to disguise, he really felt like a jerk. And he would soon feel even worse. Because for months he'd been kidding himself thinking he could marry her.

She sighed. "Well, if you really can't spare the time…" After a moment, she brightened. "Since you can't have lunch with me, I'll fix you dinner instead. I'll make Wiener schnitzel."

Wiener schnitzel was one of her specialties, and it was Stephen's favorite. "I've got a council meeting tonight, Em." The town of High Creek was the county seat, and two years ago Stephen had been elected to the town council.

Again, her face fell.

"I wasn't expecting you back until tomorrow."

She nodded. "I know."

"We'll see each other tomorrow night, though. Elliott's having a party and he's counting on you being there."

She made a visible effort to smile. "What's the occasion?"

"Hold on to your hat. Elliott is engaged."

Emily's mouth dropped open. "I'm shocked! When? And to whom? Not Charlie?"

Charlotte, better know as Charlie, Wayne was the widow of one of Elliott's oldest friends, and since Adele died, she hadn't been subtle about her interest in Elliott.

"No. Not Charlie. It's…someone completely new. Her name is Jill and he met her in Austin." He went on to explain a bit more of the circumstances, including the fact that Jill was much younger than Elliott and that she had a young son. "We were all pretty stunned when we found out."

"I can imagine. How's Caroline taking it?"

"About the way you'd think."

"Oh, wow. Poor Elliott."

"Yes." *And you don't know the half of it.*

"And what do *you* think of the bride-to-be?"

"I like her. You'll like her, too, I think." He hoped he'd kept his voice neutral.

"Now I'm really excited about the party." She stood. "Well, I'd better let you get back to work."

Stephen heard the question in her voice and knew she was hoping he'd changed his mind about lunch. "Yeah, I'd better. About tomorrow? The party starts at seven, so I'll come by for you at six-thirty. That okay?"

"Sounds good." She hesitated, then leaned over again, and kissed him lightly on the lips. "I missed you," she murmured. The fragrance she favored, something smoky and sexy, clung to her skin.

"I missed you, too."

And the sad thing, he thought when she was gone, was that he *had* missed her.

Hell, why did life have to be so complicated? Why couldn't he be crazy in love with Emily? She was perfect for him in every way. Instead here he was, mooning over a woman he had spent a grand total of five days with more than ten years ago.

A woman who was totally off-limits.

Worst of all, a woman who was now engaged to marry his brother.

Jesus, Wells, could you be *more screwed?*

Stephen swiveled around in his chair and stared out the big window behind his desk. His office was located on the second floor of the First National Bank building and the window looked out over Main Street. Within minutes, he saw Emily walking north toward her dance studio, which was a block away. She had a typical dancer's gait, graceful and balletic. What was *wrong* with him?

Regret mixed with guilt flooded him. Feeling the way he did about Jill, and knowing that he would never feel that way about Emily, it wasn't fair to keep seeing her. It would be tough, and he knew he would hurt her, but he had to break off the relationship, and the sooner, the better…for everyone.

He sighed heavily. Tomorrow night, then.

After the party, when he took her home, no matter how hard it was, he would tell her.

Chapter Six

"Why am I doing all this? I should have just told Daddy if he wanted to give a party for that woman, he could damn well take care of everything himself!" Caroline had been muttering for hours as she dashed around the house, first checking on Marisol and food preparation, then on the booze, then making sure there were plenty of glasses and plates and napkins.

She'd even made a last-minute excursion into town and the local Wal-Mart where she stocked up on paper cocktail napkins and fancy toothpicks for the hors d'oeuvres. She was torn between also buying plastic cocktail glasses and plates—after all, why should they use the good china and crystal?—and her need to put on a good show for their friends and neighbors, no matter what the reason.

Right now, because she was so stressed out, angry

and frustrated, she wanted to scream, and if Marisol, her daughter and her niece hadn't been in the kitchen and busy with food preparation, she would have.

"As usual, I have to do everything around here myself." She completely ignored the fact that both Jill and Nora had offered to help out today, had almost *insisted* upon helping, and that she had coldly told them she had everything under control. The last thing she needed was those women spying on her and trying to further ingratiate themselves with her deluded father. No telling what that other one really wanted. Caroline wouldn't be surprised if it were Stephen. Obviously age difference meant nothing to those two.

"Mom?"

Caroline whirled around. "What do you want, Tyler?" Her voice was sharper than she'd intended.

"We're bored," Tyler said. He and Jordan, who hung back a little, stood there.

"I thought you were going down to the stables."

"I don't wanna," Tyler mumbled.

"C'mon, Tyler. It's fun there," Jordan said. "Antonio always finds lots for me to do."

Caroline's gaze moved to the younger boy. *Look at him. Pretending to be such a goody-goody. As if butter wouldn't melt in his mouth. But I know his type. He's sly. He says what he thinks you want to hear. Just like that mother of his.*

Caroline was of the firm opinion that blood will tell. Tyler came from great stock, even though his father had been a huge disappointment. Still, the Conways were a leading family in this county—almost as wealthy and influential as the Lawrences and the Waynes.

But this boy—and what kind of name was *Jordan,* anyway?—well, it was obvious he came from mediocrity. She'd be willing to bet *his* father's family was even worse than mediocre. Trash, probably.

Caroline had tried to talk to her father about Jill's background, but he kept putting her off, saying things like, "It's not important, Caroline. I know everything about Jill that I need to know."

Well, I don't! she'd wanted to say. She'd forced herself not to, though. She'd learned a long time ago to bide her time, wait for the right moment before saying or doing certain things. And this situation, no matter how much she hated it and wanted it to go away, was even more delicate than others in the past had been.

She knew she had to be careful. This was the reason she'd changed her tactics and was forcing herself to be pleasant to Jill whenever her father was around. If Caroline was just patient, she was sure Jill would show her true colors eventually.

"Moooommmm," Tyler whined. "I wanna go into town. Evan's goin' to the movies today. Will you take us in?"

"The movies! I wish I could, but don't you see that I'm *busy?* Your grandfather is having a party tonight and I have to handle the whole thing by myself. I don't have time to drive you into town."

Tyler scowled.

In the past, Caroline would have stopped what she was doing and tried to placate her son. Especially since he was going to summer school to take an advanced algebra course and deserved to have some fun on the weekends. But today she put her hands on her hips and gave Tyler a hard look. "Tell you what. Since you're so bored, I'll put both of you to work right here. You can wash the front windows. How about that?"

It only took about two seconds for Tyler to decide he wasn't bored after all. "Never mind," he said, "we'll go to the stables."

Typical, she thought as she watched the boys race outside. *As always, all the responsibility for everything around here is dumped on my shoulders. And no one appreciates what I do...or appreciates me, for that matter. No one!*

She continued to grumble and was so busy complaining that she didn't see Marisol appear in the doorway to the dining room, nor did she see the housekeeper roll her eyes and walk away shaking her head.

"Take a deep breath."

Jill made a face at Nora. "God, I'm nervous."

"Hon, all of Elliott's friends will love you."

"I'm not worried about Elliott's friends loving me. I'm worried about Stephen and his girlfriend being at the party. I'm worried about Caroline acting up again. I'm worried about keeping my own feelings in check. God, I just pray I make it through the night without falling apart completely!"

She massaged her forehead; she had the beginnings of another headache. And no wonder—all she'd done since arriving at the ranch a week ago was worry. If she'd had any idea of what was ahead of her when she'd accepted Elliott's proposal...

"Jill, listen to me. You're going to be fine. You survived two evenings and several daytime hours in

Stephen's company without falling to pieces or giving anything away. You'll survive this party, too."

"That was before he said he wanted to talk to me. What do you think he wants, Nora?" Yesterday, when Stephen had said they needed to talk, she'd been taken completely off guard. She guessed she'd been lulled into thinking she was safe, that he would forever ignore their history, that it wasn't important to him at all.

But now everything had changed. Since yesterday, she hadn't been able to think about much else but how difficult it would be to face him alone. Could she do it? What if he asked her questions she didn't want to answer? Was she capable of lying to his face?

Nora took Jill by the shoulders and gave her a gentle shake. "Stop that. I know what you're thinking, but you'll do what you have to do. You're a survivor, Jill. Look at all the obstacles you've faced in the past and how you've surmounted them. You'll be fine tonight and you'll be fine when you talk to Stephen alone. He probably just wants you both to agree not to mention your…history."

"Do you really think so?"

"Absolutely."

Jill met Nora's gaze and drew strength from her friend's confidence in her. They smiled at each other and Nora let her go.

Trying for a lighter tone, Jill smoothed down the skirt of her turquoise crepe sheath dress. "What do you think? I haven't worn this dress before." To accent her outfit, she'd put on sparkly gold dangle earrings, matching gold bangle bracelets and gold sandals with three-and-a-half-inch heels.

"I think you look fabulous."

"Oh, you'd say that no matter *how* I looked."

Nora shrugged. "That's because you never look less than fabulous."

"It's more because you're my friend and know I need propping up," Jill said. But she grinned.

"I say it because it's true. Now shut up and let's go."

Nora *did* look fabulous, Jill thought as they walked from the guesthouse to the main house. Tonight she wore a gorgeous white eyelet fitted blouse with three-quarter sleeves, paired with a long black silk skirt that was slit up the front. The outfit was accented by peep-toed patent heels. All she needed was a cigarette in a long black holder and she could have stepped out of a 1940s-era noir movie.

Entering the living room, Jill smiled as she saw Sylvia, Marisol's teenage granddaughter, playing a video game right along with Jordan and Tyler. Marisol had fed all three earlier, and now Sylvia would keep the boys company for the evening so neither Caroline nor Jill would have to worry about them. At bedtime, she'd bring them over to say good night to all the guests.

"Having fun?" Jill said.

The boys barely looked up—just mumbled "Yeah" and "Goodbye" when Jill and Nora left.

Elliott had asked Jill to make sure she came over at least fifteen minutes early, so as she and Nora entered the main house, no one else had arrived yet and Elliott was the only one in the huge living room. Holding an amber-colored drink—probably his favorite whiskey—he walked toward them. Tonight he was dressed in dark gray slacks, a matching gray dress shirt, and shiny black boots.

"There you are," he said. He kissed her cheek, then

stepped back to give them admiring glances. "Don't you both look beautiful."

Jill smiled, but the smile hid a sudden ache of sadness. He was such a sweetheart. He didn't deserve to be deceived. Oh, God, her life was such a mess.

"So, what can I get for you girls?"

They both said they'd have a glass of wine and Elliott headed for the bar where Jill saw that everything was set out so people could help themselves.

"We can get our own," Jill said, following him.

"I like taking care of you, Jill." His gaze was filled with love.

Jill wanted to cry. "H-how many people will be here tonight?" she asked, more to distract herself than anything else.

"About fifteen altogether." Elliott smiled. "Don't look so worried. You won't be expected to memorize all the names."

Grateful he thought keeping everyone straight was her biggest concern, she said, "Tell us about them before they get here." Nora had now joined them.

"Well, besides the three of us, Stephen and Caroline, I've invited my good friends Bob and Suzanne Whiteoak—they own the spread south of ours. The Flying W Ranch—we drove by there on our way here."

Jill remembered when Elliott had pointed out the entrance to their place.

"And Charlie Wayne—she's the widow of Sonny Wayne, who was my best friend from the time we were kids."

"Charlie?" Jill said.

"It's really Charlotte, but she's been Charlie forever.

You'll like her, Jill. She's a wonderful person. I hope the two of you will become good friends."

Jill hoped he was right.

"And Stephen's bringing Emily Lindstrom. I told you about her. She owns a dance studio in town and he's been seeing her for almost a year now." At this, Elliott smiled happily. "I hope they'll be getting married one of these days. She'll make a great addition to our family."

"Are they engaged?" Nora asked.

"Not yet," Elliott said. "But I don't think it'll be long. She's perfect for him."

"Who else is coming?" Jill asked.

"Jim Bradshaw—he's the mayor, also an old friend— and his wife, Anne. Mark and Colleen Plummer—he's our vet and she teaches music at the high school. Jesse Conway—the two of us, we go way back. He's Tyler's other grandfather, Caroline's former father-in-law."

Jill must have looked startled, because Elliott quickly said, "He and Caroline get along just fine, which is a good thing, because I wouldn't have wanted to cut Jesse out of my life after the divorce."

"I'll never remember everyone's name."

"They won't expect you to," Elliott said. "Oh, and there'll be one more. I told you about him the other day— Pete Vincenti, the one who owns the land north of us."

By now, it was almost seven. Just as the grandfather clock began to chime the hour, Caroline—wearing a fire-engine-red dress—entered the room, and a moment later, the doorbell added its peal to the music of the chimes.

Elliott said, "I'll get the door, Caroline," and a few minutes later he ushered a handsome fiftyish couple into the room.

"Hello, Caroline," said the man, whose hair was thick and prematurely white. He gave her a hearty hug and kiss.

Elliott led the couple over to where Jill and Nora stood and made the introductions. These were the Bradshaws, Jim and Anne. Jill remembered that he was the mayor of High Creek and Anne, a pretty brunette with warm brown eyes and a sweet smile, told Jill that she owned a boutique. "It's right on Main Street. You can't miss it, just two doors down from the bank where Stephen has his offices. I hope you'll stop by sometime."

Almost as if saying his name had conjured him, the front door opened and this time it was Stephen accompanied by a stunning blonde wearing a gauzy green dress. Jill's heart skipped as her gaze met his. She hurriedly looked away.

Almost immediately, though, Stephen and Emily were headed her way and introductions were made. Jill wanted to hate Emily, but that was impossible. The problem was, Emily was nice, and genuinely warm and friendly.

"I'm so excited to meet you," she said, clasping Jill's hand. "I'm hoping we're going to be wonderful friends." Her smile was uncomplicated, her eyes friendly; it was clear she was sincere.

Jill wondered how that could ever be possible. Yet despite knowing a friendship between them would be very difficult, she felt drawn to Emily. It would be so nice to think they *could* be friends. If Jill married Elliott, she would need a friend here.

"It's very nice to meet you, too," she said. "I understand you have a dance studio?"

"I do. I opened it three years ago, shortly after I came here."

"Jill's an artist," Stephen said. "A very talented one, too."

Jill's traitorous heart tripped as she was forced to look at him finally. Even though Nora had commented on Stephen's similarity to Elliott, for the first time, Jill was struck by how alike they were. Why hadn't she ever noticed before? And if they were so alike, why was it that Stephen had the power to make her feel like a tongue-tied teenager with her first agonizing crush, whereas Elliott simply made her feel a safe, comfortable warmth?

His blue eyes, the eyes his son had inherited, pinned hers. Her heart was pounding. Could everyone hear it?

"Really? You're an artist?" Emily said. "Would I know your work?"

Wrenching her mind back to the conversation, Jill forced her gaze to Emily. "I doubt it. I'm not famous."

"She's too modest," Nora said. "She paints as Jill Jordan, and her name has been building steadily. She's especially known for her watercolors of Texas missions."

"Like the one Elliott bought for Caroline's birthday," Emily said.

Surprised that Emily knew about that painting, Jill said, "Oh, you've seen it?"

"Why, yes. Caroline loves it. She showed it to everyone after Elliott bought it for her."

Jill had wondered about the painting, but she hadn't wanted to ask. Knowing the way Caroline felt about her—after all, she hadn't made it a secret—she figured Caroline had probably relegated the painting to the trash heap now that she knew who painted it.

"Do you ever do portraits?" Emily seemed genuinely interested rather than simply polite.

"Actually, I do a little of everything." Jill had painted Jordan many times. She'd even done a bit of arm-twisting and persuaded Nora to sit for a portrait, which was one of Jill's favorites. Nora had promptly given the portrait a place of honor over her fireplace mantel.

"My personal Jill Jordan," she'd said proudly, just as if Jill were Picasso.

"Maybe I could persuade you to do one of me and some of my students," Emily said.

"I'm not Degas," Jill protested.

"I loved your mission painting and I know I'd love anything you did."

Despite her misgivings about spending any time at all with this woman, Jill couldn't help being warmed by Emily's interest.

"Em," Stephen said, "Jill might not have time. I'm sure she'll be really busy for the next few months. Planning the wedding and all."

"Oh, I know," Emily said. "But after she and Elliott are married and she settles in…" She let the sentence hang.

Before Jill could answer, Elliott approached with several other newcomers, and he'd no sooner introduced them than Caroline brought another arrival over to join the group, saying, "Dad, here's Charlie." There was an undercurrent of something in her tone that puzzled Jill.

Elliott turned and smiled at the newcomer, an attractive dark-haired woman who looked to be in her late forties or early fifties. He greeted her warmly, kissing her cheek and drawing her into the circle. "This is Charlie Wayne, Jill, a very old friend of mine. Charlie, my bride-to-be, Jill Emerson."

"Hello," the woman said, acknowledging Jill with a cool nod. "It's nice to meet you."

"It's nice to meet you, too." *Another person who has already decided she doesn't like me. So much for Elliott's hoping we would be friends.* Jill wondered if all Elliott's friends thought she was marrying Elliott for his money. From past experience she knew it was hard to fight preconceived ideas. She'd fought against the prejudice attached to single, never-wed mothers for years. People might believe there was no longer a stigma, but they'd be wrong. There was and probably always would be.

"Bit of a bitch, isn't she?" Nora murmured in Jill's ear as Charlie Wayne turned away and began greeting the other guests, all of whom seemed to know each other well. "Bet she'd set her cap for Elliott. Bet every unattached female within shouting distance has been scheming to land him, and now here you are…" Nora chuckled. "Foiling all their plans."

"Nora," Jill cautioned. "Someone might hear you." Thank God Stephen and Emily had moved away because, knowing Nora, she wouldn't have let their presence stop her.

Nora grinned. "Maybe we can start a catfight."

Jill couldn't help laughing.

"What's so funny?" Elliott said, coming over to join them in the lull between new arrivals.

Jill was still chuckling.

"I'm being a bad girl," Nora said. "I told her every woman within a hundred miles of here probably hates her because she captured the most eligible bachelor around." She winked. "Also the handsomest."

"Nora!" Jill said.

But Elliott grinned, a pleased expression on his face. "I doubt I'm the most eligible. I'd say that title belongs to Stephen, although from the looks of things, he won't be single long."

It took all of Jill's considerable resolve and courage to keep her smile from wavering as she glanced over at Stephen and Emily, who were now talking to the Whiteoaks. This was so crazy. She'd barely given Stephen Wells a thought in the past few years and now he was all she could think about.

Come on. Quit lying to yourself. He was always there, deep in your psyche, even if you pretended he wasn't. Remember the time you thought you saw him at Dillard's? You nearly fainted on the spot. You were still shaking an hour later.

"Older men are much more appealing," Nora said, her dark eyes teasing. "Of course, I'm an old broad, so naturally I would think so."

"Oh, please," Jill said, rolling her eyes. "You're not old."

Just then the doorbell pealed again, and Elliott excused himself. Soon the large room was full of talking, drinking guests. A very pretty dark-haired girl circulated with a tray of hors d'oeuvres.

"Who's that? Another of Marisol's daughters?" Nora asked. They'd already met Alaina, Marisol's oldest daughter.

"I believe she's her niece. At least, that's what I think Elliott said."

"Pretty, isn't she?"

A moment later, Emily headed their way. "Stephen's

talking to Mark Plummer—he's the vet—so I thought I'd come and join you two," she said.

Jill couldn't help but notice how the color of Emily's dress was an exact match for her clear green eyes. She was torn between envy and admiration. "Elliott said you just returned from a trip to Sweden?"

"Yes. I was visiting my parents."

"I've always wanted to visit Scandinavia," Nora said. "I understand Stockholm is really beautiful."

Emily smiled. "It is. But it's cold. And I like the sun."

"How did you end up here?" Jill asked.

"I was an exchange student in high school. Here in High Creek."

"Really?"

Emily nodded. "And since I have U.S. citizenship, after college I decided to come back." Her eyes sparkled. "And now…" Her gaze traveled to Stephen for a moment. "Now I have even more reason to stay."

"How'd you get U.S. citizenship?" Nora asked.

"My father was working in Texas when I was born. So I'm a citizen of two countries."

Now I have even more reason to stay.

Jill had thought things were bad before, but now that she'd met Emily—now that she actually *liked* Emily— they were so much worse. Because now there was one more innocent person who would be hurt if the truth came out about Jill and Stephen's past.

Because surely, if Stephen felt they should tell Elliott the truth, he would also tell Emily the truth.

I will die if she knows.

For the rest of the evening, throughout the cocktail hour, throughout dinner, throughout the after-dinner drinks and toasts in her and Elliott's honor, that thought throbbed at the back of Jill's mind. At times she was so distracted and upset at the idea that Emily was bound to eventually know about Jill and Stephen's history that she wasn't sure she could keep smiling and pretending.

Why was it so much worse to think Emily would know than it was to think Elliott would know?

That was another question Jill couldn't answer.

Or maybe she could.

But it was an answer she wasn't ready to face.

Chapter Seven

"It was a nice party, don't you think?"

"It was a wonderful party," Jill said, smiling at Elliott. "Great food and good company."

The last party guest, including Nora, had left a half hour earlier. Marisol and her daughter, granddaughter and niece were cleaning up. Jill had wanted to help them, but Marisol seemed scandalized by the suggestion.

"Miss Jill, you go sit down and put your feet up," she said. "They must really be hurtin' in those high heels." She shook her head. "I just don't know how you girls can wear them. They make *my* feet hurt just lookin' at them."

Jill had chuckled. Her feet *did* hurt. Sometimes she thought all women were masochists for wearing these instruments of torture. But no matter what Marisol said, she was the one who had been on her feet all day. And she was at least twice as old as Jill. "I'm fine. You're the one whose feet must hurt," Jill said. "Please let me help."

Caroline, surprising Jill, had intervened, saying, "You're making Marisol uncomfortable, Jill. She gets paid to do this. Just let her do her job."

"I don't know if I'll ever get used to sitting down and relaxing while someone else does all the work," Jill told Elliott.

"I know, darling, but Caroline's right. Marisol would be extremely uncomfortable to have you out there in the kitchen with them."

"Let's at least go over to the guesthouse so I don't have to watch them work while I sit."

So that's where they were now—standing outside the guesthouse and talking. Only a dim light shone through the front windows, which must mean that both Jordan and Nora had already gone to bed.

"So what did you *really* think of my friends?" Elliott said.

"I liked them." Except for Charlie Wayne, who had pointedly ignored Jill all night after having been introduced, but there was no reason to tell Elliott this because Jill had no intention of spending time with Charlie, now or ever. She also hadn't liked feeling the scrutiny of the others, who made no secret of their curiosity and, in some cases, suspicion, but she had no intention of telling Elliott any of this, either. He would just be upset, and she didn't want that.

"I'm glad you liked them. They liked you, too. But I knew they would. Anne Bradshaw told me I was a lucky man."

Jill smiled. "Anne's a sweetie. I especially liked her."

"She was right. I *am* a lucky man." Elliott put his arms around her and pulled her close. "I can't wait until we're married," he murmured, kissing her softly on the lips.

Jill tried to respond to the kiss enthusiastically, but it was so hard. She did love Elliott, but she'd finally realized that loving him but not being *in* love with him might eventually present an insurmountable problem. She hoped not; she still hoped they could marry and build a good life together, but each day it was more difficult to keep that hope alive.

"Did you want to come inside for a while?" she said, pulling back a little. She felt safe making the invitation because nothing could happen with Nora and Jordan so close by.

"Thanks, but I think it's better if we just talk out here for a bit. I don't want to disturb Jordan or Nora."

Jill nodded. "It does look like they're both in bed. But we can at least go sit on the porch."

After they'd settled side by side on the swing, Elliott said, "Stephen tells me he's taking Jordan and Tyler up in his plane tomorrow."

"Yes, he asked me if I minded. I have to admit, the idea does bother me a bit."

"I don't think you've got anything to worry about; he's an excellent pilot. Trust me, if a white-knuckle flier like me can fly with Stephen, anyone can."

Jill smiled. "I didn't know you were a white-knuckle flier."

"Flying is one of the few things that really scares me," Elliott admitted. "That…and any thought of losing you." He picked up her hand and brought it to his lips.

Jill was glad of the dark, for she was afraid of what her expression might reveal. "Wh-why would you think you might lose me?"

Once again, he pulled her closer. Leaning his chin on the top of her head, he said, "I'm well aware of the fact that you could have your pick of men."

"I'm not looking for anyone other than you." She knew this was an inadequate answer but somehow she just couldn't bring herself to say he had nothing to worry about because she was frightened herself—frightened of her precarious position, frightened of him finding out the truth about Stephen and especially of Jordan's parentage, frightened that her past was like a house of cards and any day it could come tumbling down upon all of them.

"I know you're not."

"Do you?" Suddenly she wanted nothing more than to reassure him. Or did she want to reassure herself?

"I do."

"Then why are you worried?" She had to be sure she hadn't done or said something that had triggered his concern.

It was a moment before he answered. "After Adele died, I never thought I'd find love again. And now that I have, I just want to take care of you. You and Jordan. And I'm anxious to begin."

What a good man he was. He certainly deserved more than he was getting. She raised her face to his. "You're already taking care of me, Elliott. And I appreciate it and love you for it. Very much. Please believe that."

This time when he kissed her, she kissed him back.

She also made a silent vow that she would do everything in her power to keep from ever hurting him.

No matter how much she might hurt herself in the process.

Stephen dreaded reaching Emily's apartment because he dreaded what was ahead of him. When they'd first climbed into his truck, he'd inserted a Coldplay CD in the player so that he wouldn't have to make conversation. Coldplay was Emily's favorite band. As he'd anticipated, when the first selection on the *Viva la Vida* album began to play, she put her head back on the headrest, closed her eyes, and hummed along with the music, leaving him free to think about what he'd say and how he'd say it when they arrived at her place.

He almost lost his nerve when they got there.

"Aren't you coming in?" Emily said when he made no move to open his door.

He wanted to plead exhaustion. Or a headache. Or the beginnings of a cold. But he knew she would not accept any excuse from him to cut the evening short. She would take whatever reason he gave her as a personal rejection, for what else could it be? She had been away for three weeks. Any normal guy would be in a frenzy to get her alone.

"Yeah, I'm coming in." He unbuckled his seat belt and got out of the truck. She waited until he'd walked around to her side before unbuckling hers. He opened her door and took her hand, helping her out.

She hopped down and, before he could react, slid her arms around his waist and pressed against him. "I've missed you so much," she murmured. "It seemed like the longest three weeks of my life while I was gone."

He could hardly push her away, so when she raised her face, he kissed her. When the kiss ended, he managed to draw back slightly without making it seem he was rejecting her.

"What's wrong?" she said.

"Nothing," he said quickly. Too quickly.

"Stephen, I know something's wrong. I sensed it the other day, and the feeling has only gotten stronger tonight."

Damn. She was nobody's fool. "Let's go inside, Em. We can talk there."

Five minutes later, they were settled in her living room. Stephen had purposely chosen one of the wing chairs placed on either side of her fireplace rather than sit on the sofa. It would be too hard to say what he had to say if Emily was sitting beside him. Before taking the other chair, she asked if he'd like some coffee.

Although coffee would have given him something to do, he said, "I don't think so, thanks."

Eyes wary, she sat down. Leaning forward, she said, "All right, Stephen. Let's hear it."

"I…" Oh, hell, there was no easy way to say this. "Em, you know I think the world of you."

She stared at him.

"You're a wonderful woman. Beautiful, smart, sexy."

"But?"

Feeling like a complete heel, he said, "But unfortunately I—"

"You're breaking up with me," she said flatly, interrupting him.

Hell. "God, Em, I'm sorry. I wish things could be different." When she said nothing, just looked at him in hurt disbelief, he added lamely, "You deserve someone who loves you wholeheartedly."

"And you don't. Is that it?"

"I'm sorry," he said again, knowing it wasn't enough but not knowing what else to say.

She regarded him for a long moment, then her expression changed, and she angrily jumped up. "I can't believe this. All this time, this whole past year, you've led me to believe we had something special. And now, out of the blue…" She glared at him, and yet, underlying the anger, pain shimmered.

Stephen felt a tremendous disadvantage sitting while she stood over him, so he stood, too. "I never meant to lead you on." He started to say he was sorry for the third time but it seemed to mean less each time he repeated himself.

"Why?" she cried. "Why did things change so drastically while I was gone? Because even you have to admit they did. The night before I left for Sweden, you almost asked me to marry you. I thought you didn't because you wanted to wait until I returned…maybe until you had a ring for me or something."

She was right. He *had* almost asked her to marry him that night. But something held him back—an unspoken whisper of doubt. And now that he'd seen Jill again, now that he knew exactly what it was that was missing between him and Emily, that whisper had become a roaring cacophony of sound.

"You're right, Em." He sighed. "Things are different now, but I want you to know it's nothing you did. I don't think any less of you than I ever have, and I want you to be happy. You wouldn't... Neither of us would be happy if we married."

As he watched, she seemed to shrink, just as if all the air had been let out of her body. Shoulders slumping, she turned away, but not before he'd seen the glimmer of tears in her eyes.

Stephen wished the floor would open up and swallow him. Emily simply didn't deserve the treatment he was giving her. And yet as hard as this was, he knew he was doing the right thing. In the long term, he would not have made her happy. Maybe someday she'd even thank him for letting her go so that she was free to find someone else.

"I'd better go now," he finally said.

"Yes." Her voice was thick with unshed tears.

Stephen swallowed. She looked so forlorn. So hurt. He was tempted to put his arms around her to try to comfort her. But good sense prevailed. It would be wrong to do anything more that might give her hope for a different outcome. Best to just leave.

As the door closed behind him, Stephen felt awful, like a first-class jerk. Yet he also felt a tremendous surge of relief. He hated that he'd hurt her, but it would have been far worse to marry her knowing he wasn't in love with her. And what if they'd had kids? Then there would have been a world of hurt, all caused by him being a coward.

You did the right thing.

All the way home he said it again and again.

You did the right thing.

Caroline decided to skip church on Sunday morning. She figured after her day yesterday, she deserved to sleep in and take it easy. She knew Tyler wouldn't care.

He complained every Sunday about having to go to church. Besides, Stephen was taking him and Jordan flying at noon, so if they'd gone, it would have been cutting it close, anyway.

She had just gotten up and was getting ready to go out to the kitchen for a cup of coffee when her cell phone rang. The display screen showed it was Emily Lindstrom.

Emily? Why is she calling me*?* They weren't friends. They were barely acquaintances. If it hadn't been for Stephen, Caroline doubted she'd ever have met Emily.

Yet she was too curious to let the call go to voice mail, so Caroline answered. "Hello?"

"Caroline?"

Emily's voice sounded odd, almost as if she had a cold, or had been crying. Really curious now, Caroline said, "Yes."

"Do…do you have a minute?"

"Um, sure." By now Caroline had reached the kitchen and was relieved to see coffee already made. She opened the cupboard and took out a mug.

"I couldn't think who else I could ask about this."

"Ask about what?" Caroline poured her coffee and stirred in a packet of Equal, then added some powdered creamer.

"Has…has something happened with Stephen?"

Caroline frowned. "Happened with *Stephen?* Like what?" She took a sip of her coffee.

"I don't know. It's just…he—he broke up with me last night."

"Really?" That was interesting. And wouldn't Caroline's father be surprised? Especially since he thought Emily was so wonderful. "Well, I'm sorry to hear that."

"Thank you."

"But I don't see how I can help."

"The thing is, well, I just don't understand. I thought maybe something had happened while I was gone and you might know what it was."

"The only thing different that's happened around here lately is Daddy's engagement." Caroline tried not to let her bitterness show.

"And Stephen hasn't said anything about us?"

"To *me?*"

"I—I thought maybe he might have said something to your father. That you'd know of."

Even though Caroline didn't care much for Emily—the woman was just too perfect and Caroline's father liked her too much—she couldn't help feeling a pang of sympathy. Caroline knew what it was like to be rejected by a man, especially when you didn't expect it. She was also intrigued by this turn of events. What had caused Stephen to break up with Miss Wonderful? Surely he wasn't worried about his place in the scheme of things here. After all, the ranch was half his. That could never be taken away from him, as Caroline had discovered when she'd done some research. Even if he were to move away and never do another lick of work at the ranch, he'd still continue to share in the oil revenue and any other earnings from the land, because the land had come to the brothers from their mother's family. So what was going on?

"I'm sorry, Emily, but as far as I know, Stephen hasn't said anything to anyone. In fact, just the other day my father was telling Jill how he expected you and Stephen to be getting married soon."

"He did?"

Once again, Caroline felt a tug of sympathy. Emily sounded so pathetically grateful for Caroline's revelation. Jesus, men really *were* fools. Even Stephen, who had always seemed almost *too* smart to Caroline. Caroline might not be crazy about Emily, but now that the two of them had broken up, Caroline felt safe admitting that Emily would have been a good choice for Stephen. "You know my dad has always liked you."

"Yes." Her voice was so soft Caroline could barely hear her.

"Tell you what. I'll keep my ears open. If I find out anything, I'll give you a call."

"Would you do that?"

"Sure." Caroline could afford to be generous now. Besides, women should stick together.

"Thank you, Caroline. I—I really appreciate it."

"No problem."

They said their goodbyes, and Caroline broke the connection. Leaning against the kitchen counter, she drank her coffee slowly and thought about the conversation again.

What *had* brought about the breakup? And could she somehow use it to throw a monkey wrench into her father's disastrous wedding plans?

Chapter Eight

Although Jill had been expecting Stephen's call, it still startled her when it came. She was just grateful she was alone so she didn't have to lie or pretend it was someone else. She was painting in the little sunroom of the guest cottage, and when the phone rang, she swished her brush through the plastic water glass, set it in its nest and answered the phone.

"Jill? It's Stephen."

"Um, yes. Hi." Oh, God, she was nervous. Could he tell?

"Can you talk?"

"Yes. There's no one else around."

"Good. Did Jordan have fun today?"

She couldn't help smiling. "He was ecstatic when he came home. Thank you for taking him up. He hasn't stopped talking about it since."

"It was my pleasure. He's a really nice kid. I've enjoyed getting to know him."

She swallowed. "Thank you." Her heart was beating too fast.

"Are you still planning to come to town tomorrow?"

"Yes, if...if you still want to talk."

"I think we have to, don't you?"

"Yes." The word came out muffled, and she cleared her throat. "Yes, I do."

"Okay, how about this? Can you stop into Lucy's Café for some lunch? About twelve? I'll come in around twelve-fifteen and act surprised to see you, then ask if I can join you. How does that sound?"

"It—it sounds fine. Um, where is Lucy's?"

"Right on Main Street. Next door to Anne's Boutique, two doors down from the bank where my office is located."

"Anne's Boutique? Is that the shop owned by the mayor's wife?"

"The same. Have you been there yet?"

"No, but she told me about it at the party. I had intended to check it out, so that's what I'll do in the morning."

"Great. I'll see you at Lucy's, then."

"See you at Lucy's," she echoed.

After hanging up, Jill couldn't go back to the painting she'd been working on because her hands were trembling. Instead she walked over to the windows and stared out at the river, a sheet of calm green water under the afternoon sun.

She was glad Nora had left for home that morning, glad Jordan was at the stables again, glad Elliott was down there with him, glad Caroline kept to herself at the main house. Jill simply couldn't have faced anyone right now.

If only she knew what Stephen wanted.

Was he going to expose her?

Had he decided to tell Elliott about his history with Jill? Was that why he wanted to talk to her? If so, what should she do? Tell Elliott first? Beg Stephen to keep quiet?

Nora was convinced Stephen wouldn't rock the boat because he wouldn't want Elliott to be hurt. Jill wasn't sure about anything anymore. And she was terrified.

Please, God. Please help me know what to do. Help me know what to say tomorrow. Most of all, please don't let Stephen ask about Jordan's father.

She didn't sleep well, was jumpy at breakfast—so much so that Elliott commented on it, asking if she was all right—and she was still praying at a quarter to ten when she set off for town in one of Elliott's trucks. Jordan had wanted to come with her, but she'd put him off by saying she intended to do "girl" shopping and he'd be bored. He'd easily accepted her excuse when Elliott said he'd take him into town this afternoon instead.

"We'll do 'men' things then," Elliott said, winking at Jill.

"Yeah, Mom," Jordan said. "Men things."

Jill's eyes blurred with tears as she remembered the teasing look on Elliott's face. He was so good with Jordan. So good, period. *You're a rotten person, you know that? You should have told him the truth the moment you realized who Stephen was. Why didn't you?*

But again, there was no answer to her question. Lately there seemed to be no answers to any of her questions.

She tried to clear her mind of its turmoil when she reached downtown High Creek. Even though she had the meeting with Stephen looming, she was still looking forward to seeing Anne Bradshaw again and exploring her shop.

She had no trouble finding a place to park. There was an open spot on the street across from the boutique. It was a warm morning and promised to be a hot day. Jill had dressed accordingly in lightweight linen cropped pants and a white sleeveless blouse. She debated leaving her portfolio in the truck; she'd brought it along thinking she might stop in to see Emily Lindstrom this afternoon. Deciding it wasn't a good idea to let it sit in the truck, which would probably get awfully hot before Jill came back to it again, she grabbed the portfolio before getting out.

The bell on the boutique's door jingled when Jill opened it, and Anne herself looked up from behind a glass-fronted case containing jewelry and scarves. There was an open ledger on the counter, along with a calculator.

"Jill!" Anne said, smiling broadly. "I didn't expect to see you so soon." She closed the ledger and put it and the calculator on a shelf behind her.

"Hi, Anne. Well, as it happens, I need some summer things."

"In that case, you've come to the right place."

For the next hour, Jill looked through the eclectic collection of clothing in the shop. She selected a dozen things to try on and liked all of them. It was hard to decide, but she finally settled on a polka-dot sundress, two pairs of shorts, a couple of cotton tops, and a new bathing suit. She also debated whether or not to add a creamy lace blouse to her purchases, but because it was pricey decided not to. The same went for a designer pair of patent ballet flats with an eye-popping price tag of more than four hundred dollars. For now, she was still a single mother on a limited income and she would spend accordingly. *Maybe for always.*

"Great choices," Anne said as she rang up Jill's purchases. She was wrapping the clothing in tissue and bagging everything when the bell jangled, announcing a new arrival.

Both women turned to see a meticulously groomed Charlie Wayne entering the shop.

"Hi, Charlie," Anne said, smiling.

"Hello, Anne." Charlie's gaze moved to Jill. "Jill."

"Hi," Jill said.

"It's nice to see you again," Charlie said. "I didn't get to talk to you much the other night."

Jill hoped she didn't look surprised at how friendly Charlie seemed today. It was certainly a marked contrast to Saturday's cool reception. Not knowing how to respond, she simply smiled.

"Shopping, I see." Charlie moved over to the counter where Jill stood and eyed her purchases.

"Yes, I couldn't resist."

"That's a pretty color." Charlie pointed to a pumpkin tee. "It'll look great with your hair." She made a face. "I couldn't wear it, that's for sure." She touched her dark bob, which she wore in a casual, chin-length style.

"You're a winter, Charlie," Anne said. "Blacks, whites and reds are your best colors."

Charlie sighed. "I know. But I get tired of them. And the thing is, when I was younger…like Jill here…" She gave Jill another smile. "I was able to wear just about anything. But after fifty…" Her voice trailed off. "Well, you know, Anne. Skin tones change when you age."

"We've spent too much time in the sun, that's the problem," Anne said.

"What about you, Jill?" Charlie said. "Have you always lived in Texas? Or did Elliott meet you somewhere else?"

"I've lived in Texas all my life."

"Whereabouts?"

That's why she was being nice, Jill thought. She wanted information now that she'd had a chance to get used to the idea of Elliott's engagement. "I was born in San Marcos, grew up in the Austin area."

"And that's where you met Elliott?"

"Yes."

"Jill's an artist," Anne said.

"Yes, I'd heard." Charlie's voice had cooled somewhat.

Anne pointed to Jill's portfolio, which she'd set on the counter by the cash register earlier. "She brought her portfolio to town with her."

"Oh? Can I see it?"

Jill surreptitiously glanced at the clock on the wall behind the counter. It was almost noon. She needed to get to the café, yet she didn't want to make a big deal out of leaving. "Um, sure, if you're interested."

"Of course I'm interested. Elliott's one of my oldest and dearest friends. Everything he does—and that now includes you, of course—interests me."

Jill had no choice but to stand there while Charlie leafed through the folder.

"Lovely," she murmured again and again. "I particularly love this one," she said, stopping at a portrait of Jordan painted when he was three. "And this one of your friend." She turned to a photo of the portrait of Nora that was one of Jill's favorites.

"Thank you."

"You really are quite talented. It must have been hard to decide to give up your career."

"Give up my career?" Jill said blankly.

"Why, yes. If you're going to be Elliott's wife, your hands will be full running that big place. Elliott does a lot of entertaining, you know. And traveling. I'm sure he'll want you with him wherever he goes. Won't leave much time to do anything else, I wouldn't think."

Jill almost said Elliott would never expect her to give up something she loved, but she didn't want to get into that kind of discussion with anyone, least of all Charlie Wayne. It was becoming more and more obvious to Jill that Nora was right. Charlie Wayne had obviously had her eye on Elliott—still did, it seemed—and would probably try just about anything to plant doubts in Jill's mind. Little did she know, Jill thought wryly, how many doubts Jill already had.

Oh, God, if she knew the truth about me. If any of them did....

Another glance at the clock showed it was now almost noon. Jill closed her portfolio and reached for the shopping bag Anne had packed. "Right now I don't have much time to chat, I'm afraid. I want to get some lunch, then I'm going to head over to Emily Lindstrom's dance studio. Nice to see you again, Charlie. And Anne, thank you. I'll be back soon."

Anne smiled. "We'll have to do dinner one of these nights. You and Elliott and me and Jim. Maybe Mark and Colleen, too."

"Sounds good." Jill waved goodbye to the two women and walked out of the shop.

She walked across the street to stow her purchases. After locking the truck, she glanced over to the boutique. Through the glass, she could see Anne and Charlie talking. As she walked toward the café, she could see both heads turning to look at her. She wondered what they were saying. If not for the fact she had much more serious things to worry about, she might have cared. But right now, all she cared about was getting through the next hour or so without falling to pieces or giving away anything important.

Lucy's Café turned out to be a small, cheerful place with tempting smells. A glass-fronted case held wonderful-looking desserts: cakes, pies, and cookies. There were about a dozen round tables in the center of the room and eight booths lining two walls. A pretty dark-haired woman was waiting on one of the three occupied booths and a younger woman was manning the cash register. Kitchen noises came from an open door behind the counter.

"Sit anywhere you like," the woman said as Jill entered. "I'll be with you in a minute."

Jill eyed the remaining booths. The last one on the windowless wall looked to be the most private, so she headed in its direction and sat so she could see the door.

True to her word, the woman came over to Jill a few minutes later. "I'm Lucy," said. "Menus are there." She pointed to several stuck between the metal napkin dispenser and salt and pepper shakers. Her smile was friendly. "And what would you like to drink? We've got coffee, sweet tea, plain iced tea and homemade lemonade."

"Homemade lemonade sounds great." Jill picked up a menu after Lucy left to get her drink. The menu was simple—sandwiches, salads, soups and a few hot entrées like macaroni and cheese, spaghetti, stew and chili. At the bottom of the menu, in bold letters, it said: Homemade cornbread our specialty. Served with honey butter.

Although food had been the last thing on Jill's mind, the cornbread and honey butter made her mouth water, and memories of her Aunt Harriett flooded her mind. Cornbread had been one of Aunt Harriett's specialties, too, and all through Jill's adolescence, it had been a staple of their Sunday afternoon dinners. Fried chicken, mashed potatoes, green beans with bacon and home-made cornbread.

Oh, Aunt Harriett, how I miss you. What I wouldn't give to be able to call you right now, hear that loving voice, get that sensible advice.

As always, when Jill thought about her aunt, she thought about her mother, Hannah. Harriett's twin, Hannah Jordan Emerson, had died when Jill was twelve, the victim of a botched robbery attempt in a conve-nience store. Hannah had stopped for gas, then walked into the store to buy some gum—at the time she was trying to kick a smoking habit and she'd run out of gum. She'd been the classic case of being in the wrong place at the wrong time.

Her death had devastated both Jill and her aunt. Jill's father had died of pancreatic cancer two years earlier and losing her mother, too, and so soon after, had seemed so horribly unfair that for many years afterward Jill had been so angry at God she'd refused to go to church with her aunt. It was only after Jordan was born that Jill let go of that anger and came to terms with their loss.

"Here we go." Lucy placed a tall, frosty glass of

lemonade on the table in front of Jill. "Have you decided what you want?"

Jill had been so lost in her memories she'd forgotten where she was. "Um, I think I'll have the macaroni and cheese and a small side salad."

"Good choice. Our mac and cheese is famous around these parts."

"Good."

"So…are you new around here?" Lucy's eyes were curious as she studied Jill.

"Yes, I am." Because Lucy continued to stand there, Jill felt she needed to explain. "I, um, I'm staying out at the Lawrence ranch."

Understanding dawned on Lucy's face, and she looked at Jill's left hand, where Elliott's ring was impossible to miss. "You're Elliott's fiancée. I've heard a lot about you."

"I'll bet you have." The minute the words were out of her mouth, Jill wished she'd sounded more pleasant.

Lucy grinned. "Yeah, small towns are notorious for gossip. And Elliott Lawrence goin' and gettin' himself engaged is big news." She chuckled. "Some folks took the news harder than other folks."

Jill wondered if Lucy was referring to Caroline as well as the rest of the widows and divorcées who had been interested in Elliott for themselves. She was just about to answer when the bell on the door sounded and Stephen walked in. Jill's heart immediately leaped. His eyes met hers and without hesitation, he walked over to her booth.

"Hello, Stephen," Lucy said. "I'll just get your order ready," she said to Jill.

"Thank you."

"Jill," Stephen said, loud enough so that not only Lucy, but anyone else in the place could hear. "You having lunch?"

"Yes. I've been shopping this morning."

Stephen smiled. "May I join you?"

"Of course." She gestured toward the other side of the booth.

Jill was proud of how relaxed and casual she sounded, when in fact her stomach was jumping and her heart wouldn't be still, either. She guessed it wasn't so surprising she was so good at acting her part today. After all, she'd been acting a part ever since the moment she'd realized Stephen was Elliott's brother.

Stephen slid in opposite her. "The food's good here," he said. "What'd you order?"

"The macaroni and cheese."

"My favorite. I think I'll get it, too." He looked over to the counter where Lucy was talking to the cashier. "Hey, Luce! Just double her order, will you?"

"Sure thing," she called. "Lemonade to drink, too?"

"Yes."

"So, how was your visit to Anne's?" he asked.

"Great. I spent too much money, of course."

"Anne has nice things."

Jill wondered how Stephen knew, then realized that Emily would probably shop there. In fact, she imagined the dress Emily had worn Saturday night had probably come from Anne's. Thinking of Emily, she said, "I'm planning to go visit Emily's studio after lunch."

His face changed at the mention of Emily's name.

Jill wondered what, exactly, she'd said that had

bothered him, because it was obvious he *was* bothered. "I thought I'd talk to her about the painting she wanted."

He nodded. "She doesn't teach the younger students until after four o'clock. When school lets out."

"But they're not in school in the summertime, surely."

He flushed. "That's right. I'd forgotten it was summer."

Something was wrong. Maybe he and Emily had had a fight?

Just then, Lucy approached with Stephen's glass of lemonade. After setting it down, she said, "Your orders will be ready in a few minutes."

"Thanks, Lucy," Stephen said. Once she'd walked away, his gaze settled on Jill again. For a long moment, he didn't speak.

Jill's silly heart began to beat faster again. She wanted to look away, but it was as if her eyes were locked in place, because she couldn't move them.

"You know," he said slowly, "I had a long list of questions I wanted to ask you, but right now, there's only one that seems important."

Jill swallowed. She wasn't sure she wanted to hear this. In fact, if Lucy wouldn't think she was crazy, Jill would have grabbed her purse and left. Unfortunately, running away wasn't an option.

Or was it?

Chapter Nine

"For years, I've thought about those days we spent together at Padre Island," Stephen said, his eyes never leaving hers. "I know you remember them, too."

She bowed her head. At least she hadn't tried to pretend she *didn't* remember.

"What I want to know," he continued, "what's bothered me for years, is why you took off like that, without a word. I was stunned when your friend told me you were gone, that you hadn't left any message. Why did you do that, Jill? Was that your way of telling me you didn't want to see me again? Because that's the way I took it."

Her head jerked up. "No! Didn't...didn't she tell you I had an emergency at home? That my aunt had had a heart attack?"

"No. She just said you'd gone home."

"I—I'm sorry, Stephen. I thought you knew."

He shook his head. "No."

"Is…is that why you never called me?"

"Did you want me to call you?" he countered. Out of the corner of his eye, he saw Lucy coming with their food.

They were silent as Lucy served them—first the salads, then the steaming crockery bowl of macaroni and cheese with its crusty top.

"You didn't answer my question," he said when Lucy had left them.

"I hoped you would," she said softly. Her eyes seemed sad.

Stephen picked up his fork. "I wanted to." That, at least, was honest. "But I didn't have your phone number."

"Oh. I wondered if you knew my aunt's last name."

"No, I didn't." For some reason, he felt angry with her now. Why *hadn't* she told him how to reach her? Yet what had happened so long ago hadn't been her fault, and they'd both moved on. Hadn't they? "Tell me something. Why haven't you told Elliott you met me years ago?"

It was her turn to counter. "Why haven't *you?*"

He shrugged. He'd asked himself this same question dozens of times since her arrival at the ranch.

"I suppose at first I was too shocked," she said after a moment. "Then later, it…it was too awkward."

"Yeah. That's the way I felt." Stephen began to eat.

So did she, but after a few bites she put her fork down again. "I wish I had told Elliott because I don't like keeping anything from him, but I—I don't want to answer questions about our relationship back then. I'm afraid it would hurt him and make things difficult between you two. And I don't want to lie."

Stephen heaved a sigh. "I know."

"I was afraid that's what you wanted to talk about today. Telling him."

"I'd *like* to tell him, but I'm like you. I don't want to lie, either. It seems like it would be kinder to say nothing."

She nodded, then bit her bottom lip.

Desire pierced Stephen and all he wanted right then was to yank her out of her seat and crush her in his arms. He wanted to pull that bottom lip of hers into *his* mouth. He wanted to feel her body next to his again. He wanted to make love to her, not just once, but again and again, the way they had that week so long ago. Memories surged through him like a dam bursting.

Christ, what was wrong with him? "Did you miss me at all?"

She just looked at him, her big eyes luminous. "I missed you terribly." Her throat worked. "I—I was miserable for weeks. Months." He must have looked skeptical, because she frowned. "You look like you don't believe me."

He shrugged. "You're the one who got pregnant." When she said nothing, he said, "I figured you probably had a boyfriend the whole time."

Still she said nothing, just looked away.

He stared at her. Her silence pissed him off. Why wouldn't she look at him? Admit it? "You're not trying to say Jordan's *my* kid, are you?" Stephen had considered the possibility when he'd first met Jordan, but since Jordan was only nine and since Stephen had never had unprotected sex, *ever,* he'd realized it wasn't possible.

Her face flushed a dark red. She finally looked at him. "Why would you say that?" she asked defiantly. "You always used a condom, *right?*"

"Well, *hello,* Stephen. I haven't seen you in an *age.*"

Stephen's head jerked around to see Kelly Porter, a tall, attractive blonde and Caroline's best friend, standing there. Jesus! How much had she heard? Trying to sound casual, he said, "Hello, Kelly. How are you?"

"I'm just fine." Her curious eyes swept Jill. "Hello. I don't believe we've met."

"This is Jill Emerson, Elliott's fiancée," Stephen said. "Jill, Kelly Porter, a good friend of Caroline's."

"Hello, Kelly." Jill had gotten herself under control; her eyes were calm and her face was no longer red.

"As a matter of fact," Kelly said, "I'm meeting Caroline for lunch. She should be here any minute now."

Dammit to hell. That's all we need.

"So where's that handsome devil of a brother of yours?"

"He can usually be found at the stables," Stephen said. He looked at Jill.

"Yes," she said. "He said he was going to give Jordan another riding lesson today."

"Jordan?" Kelly said.

"My son."

"Oh, yes, I heard you had a son."

I'll just bet you did, Stephen thought.

Kelly seemed about to say something else when her cell phone rang. She fished it out of her handbag, waved goodbye to Stephen and Jill, and walked over to one of the empty booths by the front windows. Stephen turned back to Jill.

Before he could say anything else, she said, "I'm going to go, Stephen. I don't want to talk to Caroline, and I'm really not hungry. In fact, I don't feel well. I think I'll skip going to see Emily and just go on back to the ranch."

Stephen felt bad then, because he knew he'd upset

her. "Look, I'm sorry I made that crack about you already having a boyfriend when you met me." The expression is her eyes puzzled him—a mixture of anger, pain and something else. He wished they could continue this conversation, but she was right. It would be best for her to be gone when Caroline arrived. "Anyway, are we agreed? That we won't say anything to Elliott?"

She nodded. "Yes, we're agreed." She picked up her handbag and what looked like a portfolio, and a minute later, she was gone.

Stephen's other questions would have to wait for another day.

Was that Jill rushing out the door of the café? Caroline locked her car and watched as Jill hurried up the street. What was *her* problem? Still wondering, Caroline walked into Lucy's and looked around. She spied Kelly immediately—she was talking on her cell phone and waving.

She also saw Stephen in another booth. It looked as if he'd just finished his lunch. Mouthing, "I'll be just a minute," to Kelly, Caroline walked over to where Stephen was sliding out of his booth.

Now that she was closer, Caroline could see that someone else had been eating with him. Not eating much, if what was left was any indication. Who had it been? Emily?

"Hello, Stephen," she said.

He turned. "Hello, Caroline. Kelly's over there." He inclined his head in Kelly's direction.

"I know. I saw her. Who were you having lunch with?"

"I, uh, ran into Jill."

"Ah. I thought I saw her leaving. What was she doing in town?"

"She said she was shopping. And that she might stop in to Emily's studio this afternoon."

Caroline was delighted he'd mentioned Emily. "I hear you and Emily are no longer an item."

He frowned. "Who told you that?"

"I got it straight from the horse's mouth." From his expression, she could see she'd startled him.

"Emily told you?"

"Uh-huh. She called me Sunday morning, in fact." She knew he wanted to say something uncomplimentary, like *why the hell would she call you?* but he stayed silent. "She's pretty upset."

"I'm sorry about that."

"Why *did* you break up with her? Not that it's any of my business."

He hesitated, then said, "It…just didn't work out."

"Daddy's going to be *so* disappointed."

"I'm surprised you haven't already told him."

Caroline smiled wryly. "That's not a nice thing to say."

He ran his right hand through his hair in a distracted motion. "Sorry. Uh, listen, Caroline, I've got to go or else I'm going to be late for a meeting."

As he walked to the counter to pay his bill, Caroline went over and joined Kelly. Her mind was churning. Something very odd was going on. Jill had acted weird, rushing out of the café like that. And Stephen had acted weird, too, almost as if he had something to hide.

Caroline waited until Kelly finished her phone call, then said, "Did you see Stephen?"

"Sure did. I also met the famous Jill."

"Really? What did you think of her?"

"Well, she didn't say much. In fact, when I walked over to their booth, it looked to me as if they might be arguing. She seemed upset."

"Oh, really. Now *that's* interesting." What could Jill and Stephen be talking about that would upset her?

"I did overhear something," Kelly said.

"What?"

"Well…"

"*What?*"

Kelly huffed out a breath. "It sounded like Jill said, *you always used a condom, right?*"

Caroline's mouth dropped open. "You always used a condom? She said *you?*"

Kelly nodded. "I'm not positive, but it certainly sounded like that's what she said."

Caroline didn't know what to make of the information. All she knew was that something really strange was happening, and she, for one, intended to find out what it was. "Kell, didn't you tell me that investigator you used when you divorced Rick was really good?"

Kelly nodded. "He was excellent. Expensive, of course."

"You still have his contact information?"

"As a matter of fact, I have his card in my wallet." She reached for her big tote and extracted a slim wallet. A moment later, she handed Caroline a business card. "Why do you want an investigator? Do you think Dale's holding out on you?"

"No, it's nothing to do with Dale. I just think it might be time to find out a bit more about my future stepmother."

Kelly's eyebrows shot up. "You think she's hiding something?"

"Let's just say there are lots of unanswered questions where she's concerned. And...for my father's sake...I don't think we can afford to wait any longer to get those answers."

Jill was shaking as she pulled out of her parking place and pointed the truck toward home. Oh, God, today had been a disaster. The conversation with Stephen had left her even more frightened than she'd been before she'd talked with him. And then, almost running into Caroline, who was sure to find out from her friend that Jill and Stephen had been having lunch together, had been the crowning blow.

Had Stephen believed her when she said those things about Jordan's father? Or was he suspicious?

Oh, God. What would she do if he put two and two together?

Sir Walter Scott had been right. Lying, even if by omission, caused the web to become more and more tangled.

When Jill reached the ranch, she was relieved to see that neither Elliott nor Jordan was around. Marisol confirmed that they'd already had their lunch and had gone back to the stables.

"They're not going into town today?" Jill asked.

"Mr. Lawrence said maybe later. I think he was worried about one of the mares."

Grateful to be alone, Jill took her purchases to the guesthouse, then sat down to call Nora.

"So how'd the big meeting between you and Stephen go?" Nora asked.

Jill gave her a complete rundown, ending with, "I know he's suspicious, Nora. I was upset when he asked about Jordan's father and I didn't do a good job of hiding how I felt."

"But you gave him a good answer." Nora was quiet for a few seconds. "Tell me, has Elliott questioned you about this?"

"Only once, and I just told him it was a painful subject and I just wanted to forget about it."

"Well, at least you didn't lie to *him*."

"Not about that, anyway."

"Jill, don't be so hard on yourself. After all, you couldn't know Stephen was Elliott's brother. As far as you knew, you'd never see Stephen again. So there was no point in telling Elliott about him. I mean, he was just a boy you met when you were a kid, someone that was only part of your life for a few days."

"I know, but—"

"But what?"

"What am I going to do about Jordan's birthday?"

"What do you mean?"

"He was born exactly eight months and twenty-four days from the day Stephen and I met. Don't you think Stephen will eventually figure out he must be Jordan's father?"

"Maybe not."

"Nora, I know you're trying to make me feel better, but Stephen's no dummy. The idea is *already* in the back of his mind, and one of these days he's going to realize I evaded his question today. Sooner or later, he'll put it all together. I just know it. And what am I going to do then?"

The question hung in the air between them.

"Maybe I should just go now," Jill said in despair.

"Go now? Go where?"

"Back to Austin." Her shoulders slumped. "I just… I just don't see how I can stay here. I can't stand lying like this."

"Jill, please don't do anything too hasty. Sleep on it, okay? Let me think about all this and see if I can come up with something. Let's talk tomorrow, all right?"

"Nora, I've thought and thought. Gone round and round. There is no solution to this problem. No matter what I do or don't do, there's no way for things to work out."

"Still…promise me you won't do anything drastic today. Okay?"

Jill sighed. "Okay."

"I'll call you tomorrow."

"All right."

"And in the meantime…"

"Yes?"

"Pray."

Chapter Ten

The following morning, Jill had just gotten out of the shower when her cell phone rang. It was Nora.

"I thought about your problem all night last night," she said. "And you're right. There's really no solution other than being absolutely truthful with both Elliott and Stephen."

Jill sat on the side of her bed. She had slept badly, and she felt listless and tired. She was certain she looked like hell.

"Jill? You still there?"

Jill sighed. "Yes, I'm here."

"Say something."

"There's really nothing to say, is there? Whether I tell Elliott and Stephen the truth or I don't, the outcome will still be the same. I won't be able to marry Elliott and Jordan and I will have to leave the ranch. So why not at least spare Elliott all that pain and just leave now and say nothing?"

"Oh, Jill. What will you do? Remember, you quit your job."

"Yes, I know."

"And sold your car."

"I know."

"And your house is on the market."

"The house problem is easily fixed. I'll just take it off the market. And the job might be okay, too. I could call Gail Leone. It's only June. Maybe they haven't hired anyone to replace me yet. And I needed a new car, anyway." At least she had some savings. Not a huge amount, but enough to cover the cost of moving her things back to Austin and putting a down payment on a car. She would have to find a job quickly, though. If her old one wasn't available, she'd soon have to tap into her retirement fund.

"I think it's a good idea for you to call Gail today. If only to see what the lay of the land is. But don't do anything else. Let me make some calls."

"What kind of calls?"

"You remember Jackson Baker?"

"The Love Bug guy?" Love Bug Greeting Cards was a contemporary line of funky cards introduced to the buying public a year earlier. Jackson Baker was the owner of the company and in the beginning had com-missioned Jill to do a couple of paintings for him. "Of course I remember him."

"Well, he called last week about the possibility of you doing a series of paintings for him."

"You never said."

"I know. I wanted to wait to see if it was actually going to happen, then surprise you."

Baker had paid well—five hundred dollars for each of the watercolors Jill had done for him—and the paintings were simple, usually just one object against a pastel wash, no more than a couple of days' work. "How many paintings would he want?"

"He was talking dozens."

"That would be a godsend."

"Yes, it would certainly tide you over until you could find another job."

They agreed that Nora would call Jill when she had any news, and that in the meantime, Jill would do nothing other than call Gail Leone. After they hung up, Jill decided there was no point in waiting; she might as well place the call to the school administrator right away.

"Jill!" Gail said when she answered.

Relieved to find Gail in her office, Jill's voice was more upbeat than when she'd talked to Nora. "Hi, Gail. How're things?"

"Oh, I'm busy, as usual. Trying to get all my teachers lined up for the fall semester. You know how it is."

"I do, and that's why I'm calling. Have you, um, filled my old position yet?"

"Not yet. I've interviewed a couple of prospective teachers, but I haven't made a decision yet. Why? You're not coming back, are you?"

"Actually, I may be."

"Jill! Why? I thought—"

"Yes, I know. I thought so, too, but it doesn't look as if it's going to work out."

"Oh, Jill, I'm so sorry. I was so thrilled for you. We all were."

"I know, and I appreciate it. Look, I'll know for sure later today or possibly tomorrow. Would…would you be interested in having me back?"

"Just say the word. I'll hold off doing anything until I hear from you."

After saying goodbye, Jill felt better than she'd felt for days. She was sorry she was going to cause Elliott pain, but this pain—thinking she'd changed her mind because she had doubts about him—was the lesser pain.

Jill took a deep breath and told herself everything would be okay.

Elliott would survive this disappointment. After all, he'd survived much worse when he lost Adele.

Jordan was another story. She hated doing this to Jordan, who was so very happy here at the ranch. More important, did she have the right to deny him his father now that she knew where Stephen was?

But what else could she do?

Jordan would be okay. He had to be. She would make sure he was. She would shower him with love and attention to make up for what she was depriving him of. And if he ever found out what she had taken from him, she hoped he would forgive her.

Tuesdays were always busy at the stables. And today promised to be even busier because one of the mares was foaling. They were at the stage now where all they could really do was make her as comfortable as possible and then just wait for nature to take its course.

In the meantime, Stephen spent the morning working

with Big Boy and some of the other stallions. Along with Jesse, one of Antonio's most experienced "boys," they exercised the horses, putting them through their paces. It was demanding physical work, but satisfying, and it helped keep his mind focused on something other than Jill and yesterday's conversation.

Jordan spent most of the morning watching Stephen and Jesse. The boy hung on the fence at the outdoor arena and anytime Stephen or Jesse got within hearing distance, he would pepper them with questions. Stephen enjoyed the kid. He was smart, polite, and it was clear he loved horses. He was just the kind of boy Stephen would have liked to have had himself.

About eleven, Elliott came out and joined the boy at the fence. Stephen, who had just finished Big Boy's workout, rode over to talk to his brother.

Jesse had finished, too, and on his way out of the arena stopped to ask Jordan if he wanted to come back to the stables and help him with the grooming.

"Yeah!" Jordan said, eagerly jumping down and racing after Jesse.

Elliott grinned, watching him. "He loves it here."

"Yes," Stephen said.

"He's a great kid, don't you think?"

"I do." Then, casually, Stephen added, "Wouldn't you think if you had a kid like him you'd want to be involved in his life?"

"Yes, I would."

"Has Jill ever said anything about why his dad *isn't* involved?"

Elliott shook his head. "She doesn't like talking about his father."

"Why not?"

"She said it was a painful subject. That Jordan's father had never been a part of the picture. I got the idea she might have gotten pregnant in a one-night stand."

For some reason, that revelation bothered Stephen. The Jill he knew wasn't the type for a one-night stand.

"She was pretty young when it happened," Elliott went on. "Only nineteen."

Stephen frowned. By his calculations, she would have been twenty. But he couldn't say this, of course. How would he explain knowing when her birthday was?

"I really admire her for raising Jordan by herself," Elliott said.

"She wasn't completely alone, though. Wasn't she living with an aunt or something?"

"Her aunt died when Jordan was only three. For the past seven years, Jill's been on her own."

It took a moment for what Elliott had said to sink in. "Seven years? I thought Jordan was nine."

Elliott frowned. "No, he's ten. He'll be eleven in December."

Eleven in December? But that meant…

"You know," Elliott said, "one of the reasons I was so drawn to Jordan when I met him is because he reminds me so much of you when you were a kid." He laughed. "As a matter of fact, he could easily be taken for your son."

As the full import of what Elliott had innocently revealed sank into Stephen's brain, his body turned first hot, then cold, then hot again. December. Jordan would be eleven in December. Jill had gotten pregnant in March. The same March of the same year the two of them had had their torrid affair.

The conclusion was inescapable.

I'm Jordan's father!

Condom or no, he had gotten Jill pregnant during that fateful week at Padre Island.

Somehow Stephen managed to keep conducting his conversation with Elliott, even as his mind was spinning.

Jordan is mine. I'm his father.

He thought about how Jill hadn't really answered his question yesterday. Instead she'd turned his question back to him, hadn't she?

Around and around his thoughts whirled. And as soon as he could, he told Elliott he was hungry, thought he'd head over to the tack room and grab a sandwich. Elliott nodded, saying he was headed to town. "I'll see you later."

Stephen walked to the main stable in a daze. Most of the help were taking a lunch break, sitting around in the tack room eating and talking. Stephen acknowledged the greetings, opened the fridge where sandwiches, drinks and fruit were always stocked, removed a ham salad sandwich, and walked out again. He passed Jesse and Jordan, who were grooming Calypso, one of the newer paints, and headed toward the far end of the stables.

Just as he reached the open doorway, he saw Jill approaching. Backlit by sunlight, he couldn't see the expression on her face. She stopped when she saw him, and for a moment, he thought she might run the other way. Before she could react, he reached out and grabbed her arm. Jerking his head to the left, he said, "Let's go over there. I have to talk to you."

At first she resisted, but when he didn't let go, she followed him around the corner where the ladder leading up to the hayloft stood. There, in a pool of sunlight, surrounded by the sounds and smells of horse, Stephen angrily studied her. "Why?" he said through clenched teeth. "Why didn't you tell me?"

Her whole body trembled. "T-tell you what?"

"Don't play the innocent with me, Jill. I know Jordan is my son. And you had no right to keep that from me. No right at all."

He thought she would continue to deny it, but she didn't. She just looked at him. Tears glistened in her eyes. The sunlight pouring into the barn lit her hair from behind, giving the impression of a halo. But this was no angel standing here. This was a warm-blooded, sexy woman—the woman who had given birth to his son.

"I'm so sorry," she whispered.

For a moment Stephen wasn't sure what he wanted more: to kiss her or to shake her. The desire to kiss her won out and he yanked her into his arms and covered her mouth with his own.

People talked about fireworks when they described kisses. They talked about passion and lust and fire. And in those long few seconds of kissing Jill, Stephen experienced every single one of those sensations. He crushed Jill to him. The kiss went on and on. Heat exploded inside him. Stephen forgot where they were. He forgot that around the corner was disaster—people who, if they saw them, would be shocked and disgusted. People who wouldn't understand what was happening. He forgot Elliott. He forgot his own code of ethics and morals. He was so lost in his need for this woman—and in his anger, his desire to punish her—that all thought had been wiped from his brain.

The whinny of a horse finally shocked him—both of them—into a belated awareness of their circumstances and the real possibility of discovery. Stephen let her go so quickly she stumbled back.

Putting her hand to her mouth, she gave him an anguished, beseeching look before a sob tore through her. She whipped around and raced for the open doorway. Seconds later, she was gone.

Stephen stood there breathing hard. His head was pounding; it felt as if he might burst.

It was only when he heard Antonio calling for him, saying, "Stephen! Where are you? It's time to call Doc Plummer. Misty's ready," that he was able to move.

"I'm here," he called, walking around the corner. He couldn't think about Jill right now. He had a job to do. In this, at least, he could be the brother Elliott believed him to be.

When Jill finally calmed down, she knew what she had to do.

She began to pack.

"No!" Jordan cried. "I don't want to go back to Austin. I don't want to leave the ranch!"

"I know you don't, sweetie, but—"

"I'm not *going!*" Jordan pushed Jill away. She'd been attempting to put her arms around him to comfort him. "I hate you!" He glared at her.

Jill's eyes filled with tears. Her son had never before said he hated her. Right now, though, she couldn't blame him. She hated herself. "Jordan, sweetheart, I know how you feel. But please trust me. We can't stay here.

I'm not going to marry Elliott, and if I don't marry him, there's no place for us here on the ranch."

The look Jordan gave her was so raw, so filled with pain and fury, she could hardly stand to look at him. "He won't want *me* to go. He's buying me a *horse!*"

Jill knew she was inches away from breaking down, something she simply couldn't allow herself to do. For Jordan's sake, she had to be strong. "I know, darling, I know. I—I promise. You can take riding lessons in Austin. I'll buy you a horse." How she would fulfill this vow, she didn't know, but if she had to take a third job to do it, she would.

"I don't want to take riding lessons in Austin." Jordan practically spit out the words. "I want to live on the *ranch*. I want to help Elliott and Antonio and Stephen. I want to ride Big Boy when I'm better. I want to stay *here*. Why do we have to go, Mom? Why?"

Oh, God. What was she going to do? She looked at her defiant, miserable son and knew this was her punishment—that all the mistakes she'd made in the past had finally caught up with her and this, her son's bewildered agony, was what she'd wrought.

"I'm so sorry," she said gently. "I know you don't understand, and I can't explain, but we have to leave. We *are* leaving. In the morning."

The look he gave her before whirling away and into his bedroom, slamming the door after him, was filled with so much contempt, Jill shivered. It was almost as if he knew she had betrayed not only Elliott and Stephen, but him, too. Yet how could he? He was only a child.

Jill told herself he would get over this. He would. The pain would pass and gradually he would accept that what he wanted wasn't going to happen. Adults let kids down all the time, and the kids forgave them. Didn't they? Jordan would forgive her, too.

But Jill had a hard time falling asleep. She had begged off dinner at the house, telling Elliott she thought she was coming down with a cold and wanted to go to bed early. Her plan was to leave before sunup. She was taking the truck Elliott had told her was hers to use whenever she wanted to. She would leave Elliott a note—she'd already written it—saying how sorry she was, but she had been having doubts about their relationship and finally realized she couldn't marry him.

I know I'm causing you pain, and I am so sorry. If there were any other way to do this, I would. But I think a clean break is best. I'll see that the truck is returned to you. I hope someday you'll be able to forgive me. And I pray you'll find someone who will love you the way you deserve to be loved.

She'd put the note and her engagement ring in an envelope with his name on it. He would find it when he came to look for her, but by that time, she and Jordan would be long gone.

She left no note for Stephen. He would know why she was gone. She could only hope he would accept her decision and not try to follow her.

Chapter Eleven

Stephen had to attend a town council meeting that evening, but he couldn't concentrate on the agenda. The meeting went on and on; he didn't think it would ever end. When it was finally over a few minutes after ten, he pled exhaustion, begged off going out for a beer with the rest of the guys and headed home.

But even though he really *was* exhausted, he couldn't sleep. In frustration, he got out of bed and padded into the living room where he plopped into his favorite chair and thought about everything that had happened that day.

He still couldn't believe what he'd learned. He also couldn't believe how dense he'd been over the past weeks. He should have realized he was Jordan's father from the very first. He knew why he hadn't, of course. He'd thought his condom use had prevented any such thing from happening. Still…the moment he'd seen

Jordan, he should have been suspicious. Sure, the boy was smaller than Tyler, but Tyler was a big kid, plus he was two years older than Jordan.

He wondered what Jill was feeling right now. Was she as rattled by the day as he was? About the way he'd kissed her?

That kiss.

It had been a long time since Stephen had been so stirred by a kiss. Ever since Jill had arrived at the ranch, he had avoided thinking about their shared past, knowing that resurrecting what he and Jill had experienced together would be a mistake. Much better to put it out of his mind, pretend it had never happened. But now, unable to sleep, tormented by his dilemma, he let the memories come.

He'd met her on a Sunday. She and her friends had arrived at Padre Island the day before. He'd been there since Friday night. He and a couple of his buddies were walking on the beach, tossing a Frisbee back and forth, laughing and carrying on. They were on their way to a bar they'd discovered and were planning to drink beer and shoot pool and in general raise some hell. It was a hot day and they'd shucked their T-shirts, tying them around their waists so they could get some sun.

Chip was the first one to spy the group of girls walking toward them.

"Hey, fresh meat," he said.

There were four of them: a blonde, a brunette, a redhead, and Jill with her cloud of curly golden-brown hair. They were all pretty, but Stephen was immediately attracted to Jill, maybe because she seemed a little shy, and he liked that. Her eyes met his several times, but each time she'd quickly look away. The other girls openly flirted, but she hung back, mostly listening, and smiled when one of his buddies said something funny.

They invited the girls to come to the bar with them and the blonde immediately said, "We'd love to!"

As they walked along, Stephen fell into step beside Jill. He introduced himself. "Steve Wells."

"J.J. Emerson."

"You in college?"

"Yes," she said. "Southwest Texas State."

"The party school, huh?"

She laughed. "I know it has that reputation, but I'm not the party type."

"What type are you?"

"The serious type." But her eyes sparkled. "Are you in school?"

"Yes, I'm a senior at Harvard."

"Wow. You must be smart."

He shrugged. "I work hard."

She smiled. "I do, too."

He liked everything about her, her slender but curvy body in the red halter top and white shorts, her curly hair, her soft voice. She was beautiful, he thought. Not movie star perfect, more a girl-next-door type. He especially like the smattering of freckles across her nose and the little drops of perspiration on her upper lip. He knew if he were to lick them off, they would taste of salt and something else, something that made him get a hard-on just thinking about it.

Before they ever reached Jingo's, Stephen knew he wanted her. And he was pretty sure she knew it, too.

They left Jingo's early. Stephen made sure he didn't

drink too much. He'd already learned booze and sex weren't greatly compatible, not if you wanted to get the sex right. And with J.J., he definitely wanted to get it right.

After leaving the bar, they walked along the beach until they came to a thick growth of sea grass. Tugging her behind it, where they couldn't be seen by any casual passersby, he wrapped her in his arms. Just before his lips met hers, he said, "I've wanted to do this all night."

"Me, too," she whispered.

The kiss wasn't gentle or subtle. He was too turned on; he wanted her too badly. His tongue plunged, his hands grasped her bottom, and he ground himself against her. Somehow he managed to stop before throwing her to the ground and taking her right there.

"Let's get a hotel room," he said thickly. He didn't want to take her back to the beach house he was sharing with the other guys. There would be no privacy there.

She nodded. After retying her halter top, which he had undone, she slid her hand in his and together they climbed up the dunes and onto the street. They didn't want one of the big hotels, so they crossed the main drag and found one of the smaller motels on a side street. Jill waited outside while Stephen went into the office to secure a room. He hurried the clerk because he was afraid J.J. might have second thoughts if he were gone too long. He breathed a sigh of relief when he saw she was still there.

They had been given a room on the far side of the unit. Stephen didn't care where they were, as long as the bed was clean. Inside, all he did was draw the drapes. The moonlight was strong that night, so when he went to turn on a lamp, she said, "Don't. I like it like this."

They undressed hurriedly, throwing their clothing on the floor. In minutes, they'd yanked off the bedspread and were in bed, wound in each other's arms.

Making love with J.J. was everything Stephen had imagined it would be and more. Although it was obvious she was inexperienced, she was eager, almost as impatient as he was. He tried to take his time. Tried to make it good for her by stroking her and licking her and doing all the things he'd read about or guys hinted about, but the moment she touched him, he was lost. Plunging into her wet softness, he came almost immediately, in a heated explosion that shook him to his core.

Afterward, he was mad at himself for not being able to wait and the second time, he made sure she was ready before he entered her. He loved hearing her little gasps and moans, loved the way she clutched his buttocks, loved the way she raised herself up so that his thrusts went deeper. And when he felt her nails dig into him as her body convulsed around him, he let himself go.

When their bodies finally calmed and cooled, they lay there quietly. He pulled her up against him, spoon fashion, and lazily cupped one breast as the other hand slowly caressed the soft skin of her belly.

Even now, Stephen remembered exactly how she'd felt. How *he'd* felt. He wondered which of the dozens of times they'd made love had resulted in the making of their beautiful son.

Thinking of Jordan and the way he'd hung on the fence today, the way he'd watched Stephen and José, the way he'd been so interested in everything they were doing, Stephen couldn't help but smile. His son. His quick, intelligent, handsome son.

Suddenly restless, Stephen got up and walked to the window. He stared out at the moonlit yard and the street beyond. There was no traffic. Everyone in High Creek was in bed and asleep.

Was Jill sleeping?

Or was she awake, too?

If he hadn't been afraid of waking Jordan, he'd call her, because he knew he wouldn't rest until they'd hashed this problem out. What kind of solution they'd reach, he didn't know. He only knew something would have to change. Because the present situation was untenable.

Jill had set her alarm for four o'clock. But she awoke ten minutes before it was due to go off. Getting out of bed, she dressed hurriedly, in the jeans and T-shirt she'd laid out the night before. Slipping her feet into driving moccasins, she walked quietly into the bathroom where she splashed her face with water, brushed her hair and teeth and avoided looking at her ravaged face in the mirror.

She wished there was time for coffee, but that might be cutting it close. No matter. She could stop on the road. It wouldn't kill her to wait. After what she was doing to Elliott and Jordan…and Stephen…she deserved to suffer.

Snapping off the bathroom light, she headed for Jordan's room. She was dreading the coming ordeal.

"Jordan," she said softly. "Time to get up, honey."

At first it didn't register that his bed was empty. She frowned. Where was he? It wasn't until she'd checked the closet, then gone out into the living room where she put on one of the lamps that she realized he was not in the cottage.

Alarm caused her heart to knock painfully. Her bewilderment quickly turned to panic. Where *was* he?

Then she saw the note.

Not her note to Elliott, which was propped on top of the mantel, but the one on the coffee table—a ragged piece of notebook paper. Grabbing it, she read, *I'm not leaving. I'm running away.*

Running *away!*

Dear God in heaven. Where had he *gone?*

And when?

She raced out the front door, stood on the porch and looked around frantically. It was hard to see much. The only lights were the outdoor lamps studded around the front of the house and along the road leading to the stable area. The main house was dark. Nothing stirred. The only sounds were the rustling of leaves, the quiet whisper of the river and somewhere in the distance, the lonely hoot of an owl.

Sobs tore through her. *Ohmygod.* What should she do?

Wake Elliott. She had to wake Elliott. He would know what to do. Like a crazy woman, she ran up the walkway to the side door of the main house, which she knew would be open. Since she and Jordan had come to stay, Elliott always left that door open for them.

She tore through the house, not caring if she was noisy, not caring about anything but her missing son. When she reached Elliott's closed bedroom door, she only hesitated for a minute. Then, rather than knock, she opened the door and whispered urgently, "Elliott! Elliott! Wake up. Please wake up. Jordan's gone. He's run away, and I don't know where."

"Jill?" Elliott, visible in the moonlight pouring

through his uncovered window, sat up in the bed. He turned on the bedside lamp. "What's wrong?"

"It's Jordan," she said, sobbing. "He's run away. I don't know where. Oh, Elliott, what if something happens to him?"

"Run *away?* Why would he do something like that?"

"I'll explain while you get dressed. Please hurry. We have to find him."

Elliott tossed back his covers and swung his pajama-clad legs out of bed. His chest was bare, covered with a smattering of bristly gray hair. To his credit, he didn't ask any other questions, just hurriedly shucked the pajama bottoms and threw on some jeans and a shirt. While he put on his boots, he said, "Tell me."

"I—" Jill swallowed, but it was no time for cowardice. "I told him last night that we were leaving the ranch."

Elliott stared at her.

"I-I'd already packed our things. Written you a note. I told him we'd leave this morning, before…before anyone was awake. He was very upset. He—" Her voice broke, and tears clogged her throat. "He told me he hated me. He said he wasn't going to go."

"Oh, Jill."

"I'm so sorry."

"Why? Why were you leaving?"

Now the tears ran down her face. "Please, Elliott. We have to find him. I know you don't understand, and I'll try to explain things to you. But first we have to find Jordan."

"You're right. We do." Grabbing his cell phone from his nightstand where it had been charging, he thrust it into his pocket, then opened the nightstand drawer and found his keys. "All right. Let's go."

As they left the bedroom, they saw a bathrobe-clad Caroline standing in the hallway. "What's wrong? Where are you going?"

"Jordan's run away," Elliott said. "My guess is he's probably holed up somewhere in or near the stables, so we're going to drive down there first."

"Run away? Why?"

"I can't explain now, Caroline," Elliott said. "But I'd appreciate it if you'd call Stephen and ask him to call Antonio. If he's gone up into the hills, we'll need to search on horseback and we'll need all hands. We could use your help, too. We might even want to call the sheriff's office."

Jill was never so glad for Elliott's calm confidence. She even felt calmer herself now, because she was sure if anyone could find Jordan, he could.

"Don't worry, Jill," Elliott said as they hurried outside and into his truck. "We'll find him."

As they drove toward the stables, Jill made a promise to God that if he only let them find Jordan alive and unharmed, she would never ask for another thing and she would never tell another lie.

Since Stephen had had such a restless night, he was only half-asleep when his cell phone rang. He looked at the lighted display. Caroline? What was wrong *now?*

He listened in disbelief as she told him Jordan had run away and that Elliott wanted him to call Antonio, then come out to the ranch to help search. He didn't ask any questions, just said, "Okay. I'll call him right now."

His hands shook as he placed the call to Antonio, who also asked no questions, just said he would be at the ranch within a half hour.

Run away. Why had the kid run away? He loved it at the ranch. It made no sense. Had something happened to upset Jordan? Stephen couldn't help remembering the scene between himself and Jill. But Jordan couldn't have known about it. He hadn't been there when Stephen had confronted Jill. When he'd kissed her.

So what was the deal?

Mind spinning, Stephen hurriedly dressed, then headed out to the garage and his truck. Twenty minutes later, he pulled into the turnaround at the ranch house. Caroline must have been watching for him, because he'd barely turned off the ignition when she walked outside. She was dressed in riding clothes and carried an insulated mug of coffee, which she handed to him.

"Thanks," he said gratefully. "Any word?"

"Dad called. He said Jordan wasn't at the stables, which is the first place they looked. He said they'd wait for us there. He thinks it would be better for us to search on horseback and he wanted to be sure we all know where to go and how to keep everyone up to date."

Stephen nodded. If they didn't have a plan, if everyone just went off willy nilly, they could be wasting valuable time. "Let's go, then."

"Just let me tell Tyler we're leaving. He wanted to come, but he's useless on horseback, so I told him to stay here with Marisol."

Lights blazed around the main barn and Stephen could see that many of the men were already there. As he and Caroline climbed out of his truck, Elliott, followed by Jill, walked over to meet them. Elliott's expression was grave. And Jill looked like hell. Even though Stephen was still upset with her, his heart went out to her. He knew how *he* felt, so he could only imagine her feelings. Their eyes met briefly, then she looked away.

"What happened?" Stephen asked. "Why'd Jordan run away?"

Elliott glanced at Jill, then turned back to Stephen. "Jill was planning to leave this morning. He didn't want to go."

"Leave? Leave for where?" Beside him, Caroline stiffened, and Stephen knew she was just as startled as he was.

"That doesn't matter right now," Elliott said. "Right now we just need to find the boy. God knows where he might have wandered to, and if he goes up into those hills..."

Elliott didn't have to finish his sentence. Stephen understood the dangers: coyotes, mountain lions, snakes, hidden traps a boy could fall into and God knows what else. There were all kinds of things that could happen to a kid who hadn't grown up out here and didn't know the hidden perils.

Stephen wished he could talk to Jill alone, because he thought he knew exactly why she had decided to leave the ranch, why Jordan had been upset, but now was not the time. Later he would make her understand that no matter what she did, where she went, she would not cut him out of Jordan's life again.

Just then, a couple more trucks pulled into the parking area and three more of the crew arrived. Elliott told them all his plan—how they would cover the vast area and how they would check in. "Keep your phones on and make sure Antonio has all the numbers."

The men went into the stables and began to saddle the horses. One by one they left to begin the search.

Elliott had told them he thought it was best to search in teams of two rather than alone. That way, if someone had an accident—which wasn't out of the realm of possibility—someone else would know and could call for immediate help.

"Caroline will go with me," he said. "Stephen, you take José."

"What about me?" Jill said.

"I want you to stay here," Elliott said. "That'll free up Antonio to search with us."

"But—"

"Jill, you're not an experienced horsewoman. You'd just slow us down."

She looked as if she wanted to protest, but she didn't. She swallowed and nodded. "Okay." Her forlorn figure was the last thing Stephen saw as he and Big Boy, followed by José, took off for the hills.

They searched all day.

It was slow going. There was a lot of brush, a lot of crevices, a lot of hills, rocks and caves. In some places, the grass was so tall grown men could have hidden.

They were still looking, fanning out farther and farther, late in the afternoon. By now they'd been joined by volunteers from neighboring ranches. The volunteer fire department was there, too, as were all the deputies the sheriff could spare. They were trying to cover every square inch, because a small boy would be easy to miss.

Jill was so exhausted, she could hardly function, yet she refused to lie down, and she couldn't eat. Marisol, who had come down to the stable area with a huge pot of chili for the men, insisted Jill at least drink water.

"You'll make yourself sick if you don't get fluids into you," she said. Her dark eyes were worried.

If something's happened to Jordan, I don't know what I'll do. Yet Jill did know what she'd do. She wouldn't want to live.

She berated herself again and again. If only she'd been truthful with Elliott that very first night, none of this would have happened. She could have gone home the next day, before Jordan fell in love with the ranch. Why hadn't she?

I'm a terrible mother.

The same two words played over and over in her mind. *Please, God. Please, God. Please, God.*

What if they *didn't* find him? What if he was hurt? What if he didn't hear them calling? What if he was bitten by a poisonous snake and they didn't get to him in time? What if he starved to death out there?

When her cell phone rang at ten minutes after five, she drew a sharp breath. It was Stephen.

She swallowed. Closed her eyes. *Please let it be good news.* Bracing herself, trying to keep her hands from shaking too hard, she pressed the green talk button.

"Jill? We found him!"

Jill sank to her knees. "Oh, thank God." She began to cry. "Is he okay? Is he hurt?"

"He's scraped up, hungry and filthy, but otherwise, he's fine. I'm bringing him back. We'll be there in about twenty minutes."

Jill couldn't stop crying. She scared Marisol, who thought she'd gotten bad news. When she finally managed to say that Jordan was all right and Stephen was bringing him back, Marisol crossed herself, then began to cry, too.

Chapter Twelve

"Why, Jill? Why do you want to leave?"

Jill walked to the mantel. She picked up the note she'd left for Elliott. "Do you want to read it?"

He shook his head. "Just tell me why."

They were in the guest cottage. It was eight o'clock and Jordan was asleep. Elliott had called the town's lone physician, who happened to be a good friend of his—of course, as Jill had discovered, everyone in these parts was a friend of Elliott's—and Dr. Hamilton had given Jordan a sedative, saying he needed uninterrupted sleep more than anything else.

Elliott was sitting on the sofa; Jill was too upset to sit.

"I can't explain." She wouldn't lie. She'd promised God, and she intended to keep her promise. "This hasn't been an easy decision for me, but it's wrong for me to marry you."

"Why? Because you don't love me the way I love you?"

"Elliott…"

"Don't you think I know that, Jill? I've always known it. It doesn't matter. I still want you for my wife."

She shook her head. "I can't, Elliott. Please don't make this harder. I don't want to hurt you, but I simply can't."

"Do I repulse you? Is that it?"

"No! It's nothing like that. You… You're a wonderful man."

"Then marry me. I'll make you happy, Jill. You won't be sorry."

"I can't."

"Is it Caroline? Is that it?"

"My decision has nothing to do with Caroline."

Elliott got up and walked over to where she stood. He put his hands on her shoulders. "Look at me, Jill."

Because she owed him so much, she couldn't refuse. She met his gaze squarely.

"Something's happened between the time you came to the ranch and today, because you didn't feel this way before. I know you didn't. What is it? Why can't you tell me?"

Seeing the determination on his face, Jill knew he would not give up until she gave him a reason he could understand. "All right, Elliott. What's happened is…" She took a deep breath. "I've… I've talked with Jordan's father."

He frowned. "Jordan's *father.*"

"Yes."

"I don't understand. When did you talk to him?"

"Elliott, please don't ask me anything more. I…can't explain it, but I did talk to him and…that has made a difference. I know now that I can no longer pretend he doesn't exist, and I can't marry you."

She prayed he wouldn't continue to question her, because as determined as she was not to lie to him again, she could not, she *would* not tell him who Jordan's father was. If Stephen should decide to do so, that was his choice. But she would not.

Elliott continued to study her, gazing deep into her eyes, and finally he seemed to accept that she wasn't going to change her mind. He let her go then and turned away, his shoulders slumping.

Jill could have cried. She wanted nothing more than to put her arms around him and tell him how sorry she was, but she knew she shouldn't touch him. Still…she owed him something more. "I am so sorry, Elliott." She was still holding the envelope with the note and the ring. She tore it open and removed the ring. She set it on the coffee table.

Elliott stared at it. "Keep the ring, Jill."

She shook her head. "I can't."

"I have no use for it."

"Take it back. Get your money back."

"I—" He stopped, then shrugged in a helpless gesture.

"Jordan and I will leave in the morning. If… If it's okay for me to take one of your trucks."

"Take whatever you want."

"I'll see that it's returned."

"I'm not concerned. Keep it as long as you need to." He finally turned to look at her. "What will you do for a job?"

"I can have my old job back."

He nodded. "That's good."

They stood there awkwardly for a few moments.

Then, sighing, he said, "I'm beat. I think I'll head on over to the house. What time are you planning to go tomorrow?"

"About eight." There was no longer any reason to leave under cover of darkness.

"I'll be up. I'll see you then."

"Okay."

He leaned forward and kissed her on the cheek. "If you change your mind, I'll always be here for you."

She was so touched, she couldn't answer. Tears filled her eyes, and this time, she did put her arms around him. "You're the best man I know," she said, "and I'm more sorry than I can ever say."

Stephen hadn't wanted to leave the ranch, but he could think of no excuse to stay. Yet he had to know what was going on. Was Jill still planning to go back to Austin?

He waited until ten o'clock that night, then he called her cell phone. When she answered, he took a relieved breath, only then realizing he'd thought she might not.

"Yes, Stephen?" She sounded tired.

Stephen had decided not to beat around the bush. "Are you still planning to leave the ranch?"

"Yes."

"When?"

"In the morning."

"You know we have to talk."

There was an audible sigh. "Yes, but not tonight."

"When?"

"When I get back to Austin and get settled in, I'll call you. You can come there, if you like. Or we can talk by phone."

"Fine."

She was silent for a few seconds. "Are... Are you planning to tell Elliott about Jordan?" she finally asked.

"I don't know." He hadn't thought that far ahead yet. "It depends, I guess."

"On what?"

"On what you and I decide."

"I don't see that there's that much to decide."

He didn't like her tone. He hardened his voice. "Let me put it this way, Jill. I don't intend to be shut out of Jordan's life again. He's my son and I have a right to see him and spend time with him."

"I—"

Before she could finish, he went on. "And if you have a problem with that, I'll go to court, where I'm sure a judge will agree with me. And then Elliott will have to know, won't he?"

"Don't threaten me, Stephen."

"The way you're acting, I don't feel as if I have a choice."

"That's not fair."

"Oh? And keeping my son a secret from me all these years has been *fair?*"

"I—"

"And don't say you didn't know how to find me, because you know that's not true. I told you I was going to stay at Harvard—study law there after I got my undergraduate degree. You could have found me easily."

Her silence spoke volumes.

It was only later, when Stephen was trying to get to sleep for a second miserable night, that he realized he might have frightened Jill so much by his threat to take her to court and the other things he'd said that she might decide Austin wasn't far enough away from him.

Christ.

What would he do if she decided to completely disappear? And take their son with her?

Caroline waited for her father to come back from talking to Jill, but when he did, he said he was going to bed.

"But, Dad, I wanted to talk to you…"

"Tomorrow. I'm too tired tonight."

He *did* look exhausted, and Caroline felt bad for him, but she was part of this family, too, and she had a right to know what was going on. After all, what affected him affected her.

"Just tell me one thing. Is Jill still leaving?"

He turned bleak eyes her way. "She'll be gone in the morning."

Caroline didn't know what to say. She was ecstatic Jill was leaving. Yet her father was suffering, and she loved him. "I… I'm sorry," she finally said.

"Are you?"

She swallowed. "I hate seeing you so unhappy."

"Then maybe you should have tried harder to make Jill feel welcome. Now, if you don't mind, I'm going to bed. We'll talk tomorrow."

Caroline felt chilled. Not just by his words, but by the way he looked at her. There was no softness in his expression. None of the kindness she was accustomed to. "Dad, that's not fair. I've been nice to Jill."

But he didn't answer—just walked out of the living

room and down the hall. A moment later she heard the door to his bedroom close with a finality that made her shiver.

Jordan cried and clung to Elliott when it was time to leave.

"You can come and visit any time you want to, son," Elliott said. His sad eyes met Jill's over Jordan's head.

Jill wanted to cry, too. She had caused so much unhappiness and heartache. The fact she hadn't meant to was irrelevant.

"It won't be the same," Jordan said.

Jill wondered if she'd ever be able to repair her relationship with her son. If he'd ever feel the way he used to feel toward her. If he'd ever forgive her.

When Jordan finally released Elliott, Jill moved forward. For a second, she considered simply shaking Elliott's hand, but the decision was taken away from her when Elliott opened his arms. It would have been cruel to refuse to hug him.

She blinked back tears as she said, "Goodbye, Elliott. Thanks for everything."

"Be careful on the road," he said. He released her reluctantly, then walked over to Jordan and helped him into the truck. After making sure Jordan's seat belt was secure, Elliott came around to the driver's side where Jill was already seated. "Call me when you get there."

"All right."

His eyes searched hers. He seemed about to say something more, but didn't. Stepping back, he gave them a small wave as Jill started the truck. As she drove down the drive toward the main road, she watched him in her rearview mirror. Her heart clutched painfully when she realized this was probably the last time she would ever see him.

As her view of Elliott and the ranch receded, she glanced over at Jordan. He was looking out the window, his face turned away from hers. His entire body language said, *Don't talk to me.*

She sighed. She was smart enough to know it was best to give him some space right now. No matter how much she might want to comfort him, anything she said would only make matters worse.

Turning her attention back to the road, she decided from this moment on, she would put the past behind her. What was done was done. There was no changing it. Instead she would concentrate on safeguarding Jordan's future and ensuring his happiness.

Yet a little voice within wouldn't be silenced.

And what if Stephen has other ideas? He said he would not allow you to shut him out of Jordan's life again. So how do you think you're going to put the past behind you?

She would find a way.

She had to.

"Why are you still going ahead with hiring an investigator?" Kelly asked. "Jill's gone, isn't she?"

"Yes. She left a couple of hours ago," Caroline said. The two women were talking by phone.

"Then why?"

"I can't explain it. It's just a feeling I have. I mean, why did she leave? What happened? It's almost like she's hiding some kind of secret."

"Even if that turns out to be true, why does it matter now? I mean, if she's gone…"

"It matters because she could change her mind and come back."

"Do you think she'd really *do* that?"

"I don't know."

"And would your father even *want* her back? You said he's awfully torn up."

"I don't know that, either." But Caroline did know one thing. She knew her father somehow blamed her for what had happened, and Caroline also knew that was unfair. She thought about telling Kelly what her father had said to her last night, then decided she didn't want anyone to know. The accusation was too hurtful.

"Well, it's your money," Kelly said.

"That's right. It is."

"So, changing the subject, do you want to go to Lucky's on Saturday? It would do you good to go out dancing and have a drink or two."

"Maybe. We'll see."

They talked a few more minutes, then hung up. Caroline immediately placed a call to the investigator Kelly had recommended. Maybe there would be nothing to learn. In that case, she would forget about Jill and hope to never hear her name again. But if there *was* something, it might be good to know.

"How're you doing?"

Elliott shrugged. "I'm okay."

"Are you?" Stephen was worried about his brother. Elliott didn't look good. His face was gray, his eyes tired.

He looked as if he wasn't sleeping. "Have you heard from her?" It had now been two days since Jill had gone.

"Only a text message saying they arrived safely."

Any other time, Stephen would have teased his brother, because only a few months ago Elliott had admitted he didn't know how to text on his phone. But not today.

Stephen still wasn't sleeping well, either. Trouble was, he was wracked by guilt. And by indecision. Should he tell Elliott the truth? If he thought it would help his brother to know the truth now, he wouldn't hesitate. But would it help? Or would it simply hurt Elliott even more?

Eventually Elliott would probably have to know. Especially if Stephen remained at the ranch. Because how could he play a major role in Jordan's life without telling Elliott the truth? But it was probably best to wait until Elliott had gotten over the worst of his pain. Give him some time to heal, then break the news as gently as possible. "I'm really sorry you're having to go through this."

"It's not your fault."

But it is.

"Something about all of this just doesn't make sense." Elliott tightened the saddle he was putting on Midnight in preparation for riding him.

"What do you mean?"

"She said the reason she was leaving was because she had talked with Jordan's father."

Stephen was stunned. "She *said* that?"

Elliott nodded. "I've been thinking about it and I don't see how she talked to him. Or when. I mean, how'd he know where to find her?"

"How do you know *he* found *her*?"

"I don't, but she originally said she had no idea where he was." Elliott sighed. "I think there's more to this than she's saying. But what it is, I just don't know."

Stephen didn't know what to say, so he just said, "What a mess."

Elliott nodded. "If you'd have seen Jordan when they left…"

Stephen swallowed. "Was it bad?"

"Terrible. He was crushed. It was all I could do to keep it together." Elliott grimaced. "He called me today."

"He did?"

"Yes. And he cried over the phone. Asked me to come and get him. Said he wanted to live with me."

Stephen's emotions were in turmoil. Between them— him and Jill—they had hurt two completely innocent people. People they loved. People who didn't deserve this kind of pain. "What did you say?"

"I explained why he couldn't, of course. I told him I loved him and wished he *could* be here, but Jill was his mother and he belonged with her."

"Was he okay when you hung up?"

"He seemed to be. I told him he could call me anytime he wanted to talk."

That poor kid.

"Mr. Lawrence?"

Stephen and Elliott both turned to see Antonio approaching.

"The vet just called," Antonio said. "I'm sorry. I told him you'd gone out for a ride."

"That's okay," Elliott said. "He probably just wants to talk about how Misty's doing. I'll call him back later."

Turning back to Stephen, Elliott said, "You want to come with me? Saddle up Big Boy, why don't you?"

Stephen had intended to go back to his office early today. He had a lot of work to catch up on, but a long ride was more appealing.

Ten minutes later, the brothers were heading for the hills. They didn't talk for a while, and partly to avoid more futile discussion about Jill and Jordan and partly because talking about Emily might take Elliott's mind off his own problems, Stephen decided the time had come to tell his brother he and Emily had broken up.

"But *why?*" Elliott said.

Stephen could tell he was shocked. "I've been thinking about it for a while. I really like her. She's a great person. But I'm not in love with her."

Elliott still looked completely stunned. "I'm having a hard time believing this. You never said anything."

"I know. I struggled with it for a long time. I finally decided it wasn't fair to keep seeing her when I knew I didn't want to marry her."

"How'd she take it?"

"Not well."

"Well, I'm as sorry as I can be. Emily's a wonderful girl. I was looking forward to having her in the family."

"I know you were."

"But…if you don't love her…"

"I don't."

Elliott didn't say anything for a while. And when he did, his voice was bitter. "Life's a real bitch, isn't it?"

Chapter Thirteen

Jill knew she needed to call Stephen, but she kept putting it off. She and Jordan had been home a week, had moved back into their little house, and she'd found a young man who, for a reasonable price, had agreed to drive Elliott's truck back to the ranch.

She'd bought a decent enough car and had also sold her first commissions to Love Bug Greetings, so she had some money coming in, even though it was still six weeks before the new school year would begin and even longer before her first regular paycheck.

Nora also wanted her to come back to the gallery, but Jill didn't want to leave Jordan. She sighed. Jordan. What was she going to do about him? He was uncommunicative and listless. At first he'd been tight-lipped and furious, rounding on her no matter what she said or did. But then something seemed to snap and now he'd simply sunk into this dull lethargy. Nothing seemed to interest him, not even the promised riding lessons. When she'd said they could check them out, he'd simply shrugged and mumbled, "Whatever."

She heard him crying at night. It broke her heart, yet she didn't know how to make things better. What could she do? What could she say?

He didn't want to go anywhere or do anything. When Kevin, who'd been his best friend the past two years, found out he was back in Austin, he'd called and wanted Jordan to come and spend the night. Jordan had refused. Then Kevin's mother called, inviting Jordan to go to their lake house with them for the weekend. Jordan said he didn't want to.

"I'm so sorry," Jill had said. "He's very unhappy right now."

And he'd been calling Elliott.

He didn't think she knew, but in the middle of the night, when Jill couldn't sleep, she checked his outgoing call list on his cell phone and saw that he'd made half a dozen calls to the ranch. She wondered what they talked about. She wished she could call Elliott and ask him, but she knew that wouldn't be wise…or kind. If Elliott felt she needed to know, he'd call her.

She was beginning to wonder if Jordan would ever forgive her. Nora told her to be patient.

"It's going to take time. You know that, Jill."

"Yes, but he's so *depressed,* Nora."

"You knew he would be."

"I know, but I didn't think it would be this bad. I wish I could think of something, *anything,* to make him feel better."

But the one thing that would make Jordan happy again was the one thing Jill absolutely could not do.

Stephen finally figured out that Jill wasn't going to call him. He decided he didn't want to talk to her on the phone, anyway. He wanted to see her. And he wanted to see his son.

So two weeks after she'd left the ranch, on a day in late July that promised to be a scorcher, he told Elliott he was taking off for a few days.

"I need a vacation."

"Where are you going?" Elliott asked.

Stephen shrugged. "Maybe Houston. Maybe Austin."

"Driving or flying?"

"I think I'll drive. That way I won't have to rent a car."

Elliott nodded. "If you go to Austin, maybe you could check on Jill and Jordan. See how they're doing."

Stephen mentally breathed a sigh of relief. He knew Jordan was still calling Elliott, and he would be bound to mention he'd seen Stephen. This way, Elliott wouldn't wonder why. "Sure. Be glad to."

Stephen left at seven the following morning, figuring he'd get to Austin around twelve or one, depending on whether or not he stopped for lunch. He debated whether to let Jill know he was coming, but decided he'd rather catch her off guard. Elliott had given him her address, and Stephen had Googled it, so he knew exactly where to find her.

He made good time thanks to fairly light traffic and a quick lunch at Burger King. It was just twelve-thirty when he pulled up across the street from Jill's house. It was located in a small, tree-filled neighborhood not far off Highway 183. For a few minutes, he studied the tidy red brick ranch house. A tall live oak shaded the front and overhung the driveway. A basket of begonias hung to the left of the front door, and a fat calico cat sunned itself on the front stoop.

When Stephen got out of his truck and walked across the street, the cat jumped up in alarm and scurried over to the house next door where it disappeared under a thick boxwood shrub. Stephen grinned. He'd always liked cats.

Walking up to the front door, he rang the doorbell.

He had just about decided no one was home when he heard footsteps approaching. There was a peephole in the door and when the footsteps stopped, he knew she was looking out at him.

A minute later, the door opened. Jill, barefoot, in denim cutoffs and a white T-shirt, stared at him. Dark circles hung beneath her eyes, and she looked as if she'd lost weight. She didn't smile. "What are you doing here?"

"I wanted to see you."

"I told you I'd call."

"Yes, I know what you said. When did you plan to do it? Next year?" He hated the way he sounded, but dammit, he wasn't in the wrong here. She was.

"I haven't wanted to call you because…" She lifted her hands in a gesture of futility. "Look, we can't talk now." She lowered her voice. "Jordan's here. Besides, I'm working."

"You know, Jill, I don't give a good rat's ass whether you're working or not working. And I'm glad Jordan's here. I want to see him." He glared at her.

She had flinched at his tone and even backed up a

step as if she thought he might strike her or something. Suddenly Stephen was ashamed of himself. There was no point in being angry. What was done was done. Somehow they had to figure out where to go from here. "I'm sorry. Can we start again?"

She sighed. "I'm sorry, too, but this is still not a good time for us to talk."

"Where is Jordan, anyway?"

"He's in his room. He… He's not feeling well."

"What's wrong?"

She shook her head. "Nothing. He's just… Well, he's very unhappy."

"Because you left the ranch?"

"Yes."

"Look, Jill, may I come in? I won't stay long. I realize you can't really talk right now, but I would like to at least say hello to Jordan. It might help, you know, if he realizes both Elliott and I are thinking of him."

He thought she was once again going to say no, but she paused for a moment, then stood aside and gestured him in.

He stepped into a small entryway. To the right an archway revealed a room that was probably meant to be a living room or dining room, but Stephen could see that it had been converted into Jill's studio. A large drawing table stood in the front bay and he could see it contained a painting in progress. There were canvases stacked along the walls, painting supplies and reference materials filled bookcases and were piled on a long table and an easel stood in a corner. Stephen would have loved to go in and see what she'd been working on, but she kept walking toward the back of the house, so he had no choice but to follow her.

They entered a good-size family room that was partly divided from the kitchen by a bar. Large-paned windows overlooked a tree- and flower-filled backyard.

"Have a seat," she said, gesturing to the sofa. "I'll just go call Jordan."

"Wait. Let's decide when and where we can talk first. Can you get away tonight?"

She seemed a bit startled, then said, "I don't know. I guess I could see if Nora would come over and stay with Jordan."

"Would you do that? We could meet for dinner somewhere or I could come by and pick you up."

She nodded. "Okay. I'll call her."

"You can reach me on my cell phone once you know."

"All right." She managed a small smile. "Now I'll go get Jordan. He's probably fallen asleep or he would have been out here by now." Her smile faded. "He sleeps a lot lately."

Stephen frowned. That didn't sound good at all. Sleeping like that was a sign of depression. "Maybe he needs to see someone."

"See someone? What do you mean?"

"A therapist, maybe."

"There's nothing *wrong* with him, Stephen. He's just miserable because he had to leave the ranch."

Stephen wanted to say something else but the look in her eyes told him she would resent his advice.

When she disappeared down an inner hallway, he walked over to the fireplace where several framed photos were displayed on the mantel. Two of them were of Jordan—one a simple school shot that looked fairly recent, the other of him in a soccer uniform. Stephen smiled. He was a good-looking kid, a boy any man could be proud of.

Next to Jordan's pictures there was a casual photo of a striking looking couple—a tall, dark-haired man and a woman who looked like Jill. Stephen figured these must be her parents. They looked quite young in the picture and very happy.

The last photo was of two women with their arms around each other. They were both laughing and looked so much alike it was hard to tell them apart.

"That's my mother and my Aunt Harriett. They were identical twins."

Stephen turned to see Jill standing there. Her smile was wistful. "I miss them."

"You look just like them."

She nodded. "I know."

A door slammed, and a minute later Jordan burst into the room. "Stephen!" he yelled. "My mom said you were here!" He looked around. "Is Elliott here, too?"

"Hi, Jordan. No, I'm afraid Elliott couldn't come."

"How long are you gonna stay? Did you bring Big Boy with you?"

Stephen grinned at his exuberance. He certainly didn't seem depressed now. "Afraid not, son."

"Oh, man." His face fell. "I was hoping we could go riding."

"I know a couple of great places around here where we could ride. Maybe your mother would let me take you to one of them tomorrow."

The boy's eyes widened. "Mom! Can I? Can I?"

"Jordan, calm down, okay? And yes, I guess you may go if Stephen doesn't mind taking you."

"Oh, boy! What time tomorrow? Can we go early?"

Stephen chuckled. "We'll go as early as they'll let us in. Tell you what. I'll get all the information and talk to your mother later about what time you should be ready."

They talked for a few more minutes, then Stephen said he had to be going. "Call me after you talk to Nora," he reminded Jill.

"I said I would."

To Jordan, Stephen said, "I'll check on those stables when I get to my hotel."

Jordan's eyes were shining as they said goodbye. Stephen smiled at Jill and, although she didn't seem nearly as happy about him being there as her son was— *their* son was—she returned his smile.

As Stephen drove to a nearby Fairfield Inn he'd seen on his way to Jill's, he couldn't help thinking about how great it was going to be to have Jordan in his life. There were so many things they could share, so many things he could teach the boy. Riding was only the beginning. Stephen could take him fishing and teach him to fly, they could go camping and on ski trips and to places like Disneyland, New York and Washington, D.C.

Stephen was thrilled to know he had a son—someone to carry on the Wells family name. These changes would take a while, he knew that. There'd have to be a period of adjustment, but once they told Jordan that Stephen was his father, surely Jill would agree to let Stephen take the legal steps necessary to change Jordan's birth certificate so that his true parentage was reflected.

Thinking of all the future might hold, he promised

himself he would do nothing to upset Jill tonight. Because after seeing Jordan again, he felt more strongly than ever that he wanted to play an active role in the boy's life, and he did not want to have to go to court as Jill's adversary to accomplish it.

"So he finally showed up," Nora said when Jill called her.

"What do you mean, *finally?*"

"Frankly, Jill, I thought you'd see him here a lot sooner than this. How'd Jordan react to seeing him?"

"Like the old Jordan. It actually hurt to see how happy he was." Jill wondered if her son would ever be that happy with just her again.

"In that case, maybe he'd like to come to my place tonight instead of me coming there. Tell him I'll take him for Mexican food and to see that new Pixar movie. I'll get Vivian to close for me." Vivian was Nora's new assistant.

"Let me ask him right now." Jill walked to Jordan's room and was relieved to find his bedroom door open. Lately he'd kept it shut against her all the time. He was sitting at his computer playing a game and turned when she tapped on his door frame. "Honey, Nora wants to know if you'd like to go out for Mexican food tonight, then to see that new Pixar movie."

"Are you going, too?" he asked pointedly, with unconcealed mistrust.

"No. I'm going out with Stephen because we need to talk about some things. Like you going to the ranch to visit."

His face lit up. *"Really?"*

Jill smiled. "Yes, really."

"Okay. Ask Nora if we can go to Rosa's."

Jill called Nora back right away. "He said okay, Nora. And he's put in his order for Rosa's."

Nora laughed. "Great. That's my favorite restaurant, too."

"Do you want me to drop him at the gallery?" Jill asked. "Save you some time?"

"If you want to, sure."

Jill looked at her watch. It was just one-thirty. After thinking for a minute, she said, "How about if I drop him off about four?"

"Perfect. We can have an early dinner and make the seven o'clock movie."

As they talked, Jill walked back to the privacy of her studio. "I'm nervous about tonight," she admitted.

"Yeah, well, you should be."

"*You're* a big help!"

"Just be careful, okay?"

"I will."

"Don't bring him back to the house."

"Nora!"

"Sorry, but I don't want to see you get hurt again. Bad enough Elliott is suffering."

"I know. Trust me, I won't do anything stupid. I learned my lesson."

Because Nora was such a good friend, she didn't remind Jill of the fact she'd *already* done something stupid in allowing Stephen to kiss her the way she did. Why did he have this effect on her? Why was she so helpless to resist him?

After she and Nora hung up, she kept thinking about that episode in the stables. Her face burned as she remembered the way she'd behaved. Instead of shoving him away, as she *should* have done, she'd practically melted into his arms. In fact, if he'd thrown her down onto the floor that day and torn her clothes off, she probably would have let him.

But why was she surprised? It had been that way from the moment she met him all those years ago. Whatever he'd wanted, she'd happily supplied. She'd had no experience with that kind of desire and passion, but it hadn't stopped her. In fact, she'd been wanton. They'd spent so much time having sex that week, it was a wonder they'd remembered to do anything else.

Was she going to be able to handle having Stephen around? Coming to the house to see Jordan? Could she keep her emotions in check, not let him get to her again?

She had to.

Because no matter how she felt, there could never be any future between them. She knew it and he knew it, too. Not that he had acted like he *wanted* a future with her. But if he *did*, it would still be impossible. Because they could never ignore the fact of Elliott's existence.

No matter that Elliott was a wonderful, caring and generous man who loved both of them. Well, Elliott *had* loved her…before. Maybe he no longer did. She hoped he no longer did. She hated that she'd hurt him; she wanted him to heal quickly.

But whether he still loved her or not was irrelevant. She could never be with Elliott. And she could never be with Stephen, even if Stephen wanted her. The most they could ever have was some kind of sordid, hidden relationship. One that, if exposed, would cause more damage and could never be repaired.

A terrible secret had led to this heartache, and now there was no way out. There were only two choices: to forever conceal their history from Elliott and Jordan, or to tell them both everything as soon as possible.

A terrible lie or a terrible truth.

Chapter Fourteen

Caroline wished she knew what to do. Her father was a wreck; that was apparent to anyone with eyes. She hadn't seen him like this since her mother had died. Damn that Jill. Why'd she have to come into their lives, anyway?

Caroline still couldn't figure out why she'd left. Her father had been totally close-mouthed about the situation, and Stephen certainly hadn't had anything to say. The one time she'd asked him if he knew what was at the bottom of the breakup, he'd given her a cold look and said, "Ask your father if you want to know, Caroline. Not me."

She gritted her teeth, remembering the disdainful way he'd dismissed her concerns. Sometimes she despised Stephen.

She sighed heavily. Her father was avoiding her. He was gone by the time she got up in the morning and had taken to having his lunch with the crew at the stables. The only time she saw him was at dinner, because after dinner he either went back to the stables or he went directly into his room where presumably he read or watched TV alone.

In some ways, things had been much better while Jill was there. Despite this, Caroline didn't want her back. Her father would get over this. Sure, you thought you were going to die when the person you loved dumped you, but you didn't. You eventually got over it. Caroline should know; she'd been through it herself.

She just had to wait this out. Her father would come around again, be his old self. It would just take time.

But in the meantime…

Maybe it was better to stay out of his way.

Jill dressed carefully, even though she told herself this was *not* a date. This was a dinner of necessity where she and Stephen would—like sensible, civilized adults— talk about Jordan's future and how much a part of that future Stephen would play.

Even so, she took extra care with her hair and her makeup, using concealer to hide the circles under her eyes. And even though her clothes were casual, her short denim skirt was flattering and her lined, white lace tee emphasized her tan. She slipped her feet into espadrilles, slung her big straw bag over her shoulder and headed out.

She and Stephen had made arrangements to meet at the restaurant—a neighborhood Italian place Jill liked, not just for the food but because it was quiet and you could talk without shouting. Stephen had offered to come by and pick her up, but she'd said she preferred to drive herself. No way did she want to be tempted to invite him in when they returned home. Jordan was spending the night at Nora's, so her safety buffer would be gone. Best to play it safe.

She arrived at the restaurant a few minutes after seven and found Stephen already there and waiting for her. Her heart tripped at the sight of him. "I didn't keep you waiting long, I hope."

He smiled and shook his head. "I just got here." He gave her an appreciative look.

She was glad she'd taken the trouble to look her best. After all, whether they had a relationship or not was beside the point. A woman always wanted to look good. Speaking of looking good, Stephen was no slouch in that department. In jeans and a pale blue T-shirt, he was casually sexy, the kind of man who always drew interested glances from women. Even now the hostess was eyeing him, and Jill had the entirely inappropriate impulse to put a possessive arm through his.

Stop that! He's not yours and he never will be. And this is not a date. How many times do you have to remind yourself of that?

They didn't try to make conversation until they were seated, had placed their orders and gotten their drinks— a glass of the house wine for each of them.

"To fresh beginnings," Stephen said then, raising his glass.

Jill touched her glass to his and drank some of her wine. She tried to still the nervous butterflies in her stomach. She didn't know why she felt so nervous— Stephen was a perfect gentleman and although he *had* given her an admiring glance when she arrived, now he was simply pleasant, as if they were no more than casual friends. *As if that kiss in the barn hadn't happened.* She wasn't ready to admit that his pretending it hadn't happened bothered her. After all, *she* was pretending it hadn't happened, either. And wasn't that best? What good would come of talking about that kiss? Since there could never be another. Never *would* be another. It had been a mistake, one they couldn't repeat.

She mentally sighed. Yes. That was the bottom line, wasn't it? The kiss was an aberration. Something that had happened in the heat of his shock and rage over her keeping Jordan's existence from him. Now that he had calmed down, now that they'd both calmed down, he realized, as she did, that they could never share more than the parentage of their son. And he was acting accordingly. As she must.

He set his glass down, met her eyes. "Was Jordan okay after I left?"

"Yes, he was fine." She smiled. "Happy and looking forward to tomorrow."

He smiled, too. "Good."

She'd always loved his smile. Warm and genuine, it softened the planes of his face and crinkled the corners of his eyes. To stop her thoughts from going in a dangerous direction, she took another drink of her wine. "I know you must have questions," she finally said.

He nodded. "Yeah, I'm curious about a couple of things."

"What are they?"

"I've been wondering…didn't you have to put something on Jordan's birth certificate about his father?"

"Yes."

"So what did you put?"

"I…" She took a deep breath. "I said his father was unknown."

He stared at her. "And that didn't bother you?"

She squirmed under his unswerving gaze. "What do you mean?"

"Lying like that? Having him carry the stigma of an 'unknown' father? Didn't you have to produce a birth certificate when he started school?" The warmth and friendliness he'd displayed so far had disappeared. Now he sounded like a prosecutor questioning a hostile witness. Even his eyes had darkened.

She forced her voice not to waver. "Look, Stephen, I know you're angry. But put yourself in my position. I couldn't have your name put on the birth certificate. Not when I had no idea if I'd ever see you again."

"So you lied instead."

"That's not fair."

"What's not fair about it? Besides, I told you before, Jill. You could have found me if you'd really wanted to."

Jill wanted to dispute this. She wanted to say that she'd had no idea how to get in touch with him. But that wasn't true and they both knew it. She could have tracked him down at Harvard. The truth was, she was scared to contact him. Scared he wouldn't want to have anything more to do with her. Scared he would deny any responsibility. Or if he did, that he would push her to have an abortion. Or if not that, scared he would make trouble for her. And if she was finally being honest with herself, maybe deep down, she hadn't wanted to share her child. But she said none of this. Instead she looked down at her hands, which were gripping her napkin in her lap. She was on the verge of tears and she knew she had to get her emotions under control. Tears were weak, and if ever she needed to remain strong, it was here and now, with this man.

"What have you told Jordan when he asked about me?" Stephen said. "Did you lie to him, too?"

Jill looked up, started to answer, but their waiter was approaching with their salads and a basket of bread, so she fell silent. She was glad of the extra time, because she'd managed to regain her composure by the time he left them alone again and was able to reply to Stephen's question quietly and with dignity. "I told him the truth."

"Oh? What, exactly, did you say?"

She hated the way he was looking at her. As if she was someone he didn't like very much. She lifted her chin, determined not to let him see how much his attitude bothered her. "I told him his father was a nice man I had met when I was very young and that he…you…had never known about him." Jill speared a piece of tomato from her salad and ate it, more to give herself something to do than because she was hungry.

"And he accepted that?"

"He seemed to. You have to understand…many of the children in Jordan's school come from single-parent households, so it's not uncommon for the fathers, especially, to be absent."

"Christ, what a world we live in." He shook his head. Gazed off into space for a minute. When he finally met her eyes again, his anger seemed to have faded. "And he only asked about me that one time?"

Jill nodded, moved by the wistful expression on his

face. "But he's talked about the fathers of a couple of his friends and I know from what he's said that he's missed having…you in his life." That was hard for her to admit, but Stephen deserved to hear it, even if it made him angrier with her than he already was.

"I want that to change."

"I know you do. I—I want that, too."

"You realize that in order for that to happen, Elliott will have to know."

"Yes," she said quietly. "I do."

Stephen finally began to eat his salad. "It would be ideal if we could tell him together, but I think it would be easier on him if I talked to him first. Don't you?"

"I do."

"He may want to talk to you later, though."

"Or he may never want to talk to me again," said Jill sadly.

"Elliott's not like that, Jill."

"I know he's not. But he would certainly be justified if he felt that way."

"Now you're being too hard on yourself. You couldn't have known I was his brother when you came to the ranch."

"No, but—"

She stopped and they both fell silent as their waiter arrived with their entrées. "Didn't you like the salad?" he said, eyeing their plates, both of which were still at least half full.

"We just got busy talking," Stephen said.

The waiter served them—lasagna for Stephen, tortellini for Jill—then refilled their water glasses, asked if they'd like more wine and finally left them alone.

"Maybe we'd better eat," Stephen said. "Then we can talk some more."

"Okay."

Jill always ate slowly, so Stephen was nearly finished with his meal when she was only halfway through hers. Deciding she would take the rest home to have for lunch tomorrow, she pushed her plate away. "How *do* you think Elliott will react when you tell him about Jordan?"

"I'm not sure. I know he'll be shocked."

"Do you think he'll be angry?"

"He might be angry that we didn't tell him about our past relationship right away." Stephen finished off his wine. "And frankly, I wouldn't blame him for being furious. We *should* have told him. If we had, this news about me being Jordan's father wouldn't be so shocking."

"Do…do you think he will still want Jordan to come and visit?" Jordan would be crushed if Elliott no longer wanted him around.

"Elliott would never take his disappointment and pain out on Jordan. If you think he would, you don't know Elliott as well as I thought you did."

Jill knew Stephen was right and was ashamed of herself for even *thinking* Elliott would be vindictive. She sighed. If only she'd had the courage to face up to the truth earlier. "So when will you tell him?"

"As soon as I go back."

"Which will be?"

"Day after tomorrow. I want to keep my promise to Jordan, take him riding tomorrow, then maybe take him out to dinner tomorrow night—if that's okay with you?"

"That's fine."

"Then I'll leave the next morning."

"You're not planning to tell Jordan right away, are you?"

"I think we should tell him together, but I want to wait until he's had a chance to get used to being with me one on one."

Jill breathed a sigh of relief. Despite his justifiable anger with her, Stephen was going to be reasonable.

They talked awhile more, mostly about how often Stephen could see Jordan. Jill told him he could see the boy as often as he wanted, at least through the end of the summer. "Once school starts, it will be more difficult, because he'll be awfully busy."

"I'd still like to spend two weekends a month with him. I'll come to Austin if I have to, but I know he'd enjoy being in High Creek a lot more."

"I'm sure you're right," she said sadly. Her life would be very different from now on. The changes might be better for Jordan, but they would be much lonelier for her. It would be different if she was looking forward to a future with Stephen, too. But of course, she wasn't. And even though she knew this was best, she couldn't help the feeling of desolation that gripped her. The unspoken fear that once her son knew Stephen was his father, that his adored Elliott was his uncle, that he, Jordan, had a legitimate place at the ranch he loved— she and Jordan would never be close again. His love and loyalty would be transferred to the father and heritage she had denied him for so long, and she would forevermore be on the outside looking in.

As if he knew what she was thinking and feeling, Stephen's eyes softened, and he reached across the table to take her hand, but before he could, she put it into her lap. The last thing she needed right now was sympathy…or Stephen's touch. Either one might do her in. And she couldn't, she simply *couldn't* allow herself to become emotional. Emotions led to impulsive actions, actions she knew she would regret.

"If you don't mind, I'd like to go now," she said. "Would you get the check? I'm going to the restroom." Grabbing her purse, she slid out of the booth.

In the restroom, she stared at her face in the mirror. Despite her tan, her face looked pale, her eyes huge and troubled. She took long breaths and told herself to calm down.

You won't lose Jordan. He's gaining a father. That's all.

Continuing to reassure herself, she washed her hands, touched up her lipstick, and rubbed a bit into her cheeks to give them some color. Then she fluffed her hair, took a couple more deep breaths and returned to their booth.

Stephen had just finished signing the charge slip and stood at her arrival. His eyes were concerned as they studied her. Jill smiled and lifted her chin, saying, "Ready?" brightly to show him she was fine.

He placed his hand lightly at her waist as he guided through the maze of tables and out into the sultry night. Sometimes Austin did a good job of pretending to be Houston, Jill thought, with more humidity than its location touted, and tonight was one of those times.

As they approached her car, Jill said, "What time are you planning to pick up Jordan in the morning?"

"How does nine o'clock sound?"

Jill cringed inwardly. Because of morning traffic, to have him home and ready to go by nine, she'd have to get to Nora's house no later than eight. "That's fine."

She put out her right hand. "Thanks for dinner. I'll see you in the morning."

After a second's hesitation during which she actually thought he might try to kiss her, which was, of course, ridiculous, he took her hand and held it. "Good night, Jill," he said softly.

Jill was glad it was dark. Absurdly, she felt like crying again. Or worse—throwing her arms around him and pressing herself close. God. What was *wrong* with her? Did she never learn?

Freeing her hand, she groped in her purse, found her keys, and unlocked the driver's side door of her car. Stephen backed away so that she would have room to pull out of her parking slot, but he didn't head toward his truck, and she realized he was going to stand there and watch until she was safely on her way.

She inserted her key in the ignition and put her foot on the gas. Nothing happened. Once again, she turned the key and pressed down on the gas. Nothing. Just a grinding noise.

Jill closed her eyes. It sounded as if her battery was dead. Now she really *did* feel like crying.

By now Stephen had walked around to the driver's side and she lowered the window.

"Sounds like your battery is dead," he said.

She sighed. "I know." *Stupid, stupid car.*

"I have some jumper cables. I'll give you a jump."

Five minutes later, her car's engine was humming away.

"I'll follow you home," Stephen said as he removed the cables.

"That's not necessary."

"I know it's not necessary, but I want to be sure you

get home safely. Besides, my hotel isn't that far from your house, so it's not going to take me out of my way."

Jill knew it would sound ungrateful to protest. And she had to admit, it did feel good to know he was right behind her in case something else should go wrong.

When she reached her house, she pulled into the driveway and pressed her garage door opener so she could go straight into the garage. When she got out of her car, she saw that Stephen had parked in the driveway. He exited his truck and walked toward her.

"How long have you had that battery?" he said.

"I have no idea. I just bought this car."

"You need to call the dealer you bought it from. The battery shouldn't be dying on you."

"I intend to. I'll call them tomorrow morning."

They stood there awkwardly. Jill desperately wanted to go into the house, because the longer she was in Stephen's company, the harder it was to remain in control. "Well," she said, "thanks for everything." *Please turn around. Please say good night and go.*

"No problem." He didn't move.

What should she do? She could hardly walk to the door and leave him standing there.

"Jill…" He reached out.

Jill jerked back, nearly stumbling, she'd moved so fast. "I—I have a terrible headache, Stephen. I've… I've got to go in. I'll see you in the morning." And then she *did* bolt. She didn't wait for him to answer. She simply turned tail, walked as fast as she could without running to the back door, unlocked it and went inside.

Her heart was pounding. She had no idea if he was still standing there or if he'd finally turned and gotten back into his truck. Oh, God. What must he be thinking? She'd acted like a lunatic. So much for being calm, cool and collected.

And then she heard the sound of his truck starting.

Sinking to the floor, she buried her head in her hands and let the tears come.

Chapter Fifteen

"Caroline, I've been thinking."

Caroline froze, fork halfway to her mouth. Her father's tone seemed ominous, maybe because he'd hardly spoken to her since Jill left.

Finished eating, he wadded up his napkin, put it on his plate and sat back. "And what I think is that it's time for you to find a place of your own."

Caroline put her fork down. Her heart was thudding.

"After all," he continued, and now his voice was gentler, and he actually looked at her affectionately instead of with the hard gaze she'd come to expect lately. "It's been four years."

"Yes, I know." She couldn't believe how frightened she felt. And at her father's hands! Her father! The man who had always been her protector, the one person she could always count on, the person who loved her, no matter what.

And now he was throwing her out.

"Sweetheart, don't look at me like that. It *is* time. You know it is. It'll be a lot better for you *and* for Tyler to have your own place. It's not healthy for you to live here with me."

"But why not? I—I love being here on the ranch. I know. What if Tyler and I move into the guest cottage? That way I'll *have* my own place and you'll have yours."

"No."

Caroline stared at him.

"Moving into the guesthouse would simply be more of the same. You need to be independent. So what I suggest is that you call Nancy Ellis and tell her to start looking for a place you can buy. Maybe a place with a bit of land so you can keep a horse on the property."

He didn't even want her to *ride* at the ranch anymore?

"Not that you won't always be welcome to ride here," he added quickly, "but it's not the same as having your horse close by."

Caroline could feel herself trembling. Her eyes filled with tears, and that fact alone shocked her. She never cried. "I knew you blamed me for Jill," she said bitterly.

Her father sighed heavily. "This isn't about Jill. We should have had this talk a long time ago. Two years ago, in fact. But I kept putting it off because I didn't want to hurt you."

"And now you don't care if you hurt me."

"That's not true. I love you. And I want the best for you."

Caroline wanted to say if that was true he wouldn't be throwing her out like the trash.

"Caroline, someday you'll look back on this and realize getting your own place *is* the best thing for you. And to make it easier for you, I'll even give you the down payment."

"I don't need money. I have plenty of my own. You know that."

"It would give me pleasure to provide the down payment."

You mean it would assuage your guilt! But before she could answer aloud, the phone rang. Not her cell phone, the house phone. Automatically, she started to rise, but her father said, "I'll get it."

"Hello?" he said. Then, smiling, "Oh, hello, Charlie. How are you?"

Caroline didn't know what to do. If only that stupid investigator had found something incriminating about Jill, something she could have used to show her father that Jill would have eventually let him down, anyway, no matter what Caroline did or didn't do. Besides, what had she *done?* Why was he punishing her? He could say anything he wanted about Jill having nothing to do with him asking her to move, but she knew that wasn't true.

She glanced at her father, who had moved out of the kitchen and into the hallway. He was still talking to Charlie and he seemed to be enjoying the conversation. "Thanks," he was saying. "I'll look forward to it. Can I bring anything? No? Well, I'll at least bring a couple of bottles of wine."

Caroline didn't know whether to leave or stay. He

talked a few minutes more, then said, "Thanks again, Charlie. See you Saturday night."

Walking back into the kitchen, he replaced the phone in its base, then leaned against the counter and looked at her. "So what have you decided? Do you want me to help you find a house?"

Caroline had never felt so helpless in her life. What could she say or do to change his mind? She shrugged. "I don't know. I—I have to think about it."

"All right then. But the offer's open. If you want me to tag along when you start looking, I'll be happy to. Just give me some notice." And with that, he walked over, kissed her on the cheek and left the kitchen.

Jill wanted to talk to Nora about her dinner with Stephen, but she couldn't talk freely in front of Jordan, so she told Nora she'd call her later.

Nora nodded her understanding. "Bye, Jordan. Last night was fun."

"Bye," Jordan said.

"And?" Jill prompted.

Jordan grinned. "And thanks!"

Later, after Jordan and Stephen left to go riding, Jill called the gallery. "Can you talk?" she said when Nora answered.

"Yes. It's slow this morning. Tell me everything."

So Jill launched into a blow-by-blow account of the dinner. When she finished, she said, "What do you think?"

"I think Stephen is a terrific guy and he's going to make Jordan a wonderful father."

"Yes, I do, too, but…"

"But what? Are you still worried about Elliott and what his reaction will be?"

"Well, yes, but there's something else." She sighed. "Do you think Jordan will hate me when he finds out?"

"No, I don't think he'll hate you. Frankly, I think he'll be thrilled."

"You do?"

"Yes. If he were older—say in his teens—then you might get a different reaction. But Jordan's still young enough that I don't think he'll realize all the ramifications."

"I hope…" Oh, shoot. If she gave voice to her worst fear, Nora would probably think a lot less of her.

"Something else is bothering you."

"Yes."

"Let me guess. You're worried Jordan's going to be *so* thrilled about Stephen and the ranch and Elliott, too, that he's going to want to spend more and more time there and less and less time with you."

"Yes," Jill whispered.

"Ah, Jill. I knew you were thinking about that, and the truth is, I don't blame you. It *is* a possibility, especially *because* Jordan is as young and impressionable as he is. But he knows you love him and he knows how hard you've worked to give him a good life and eventually that will all fall into place for him."

"Maybe that would be true if Stephen had abandoned us, but remember, *I'm* the one who kept them apart. Jordan might not think about that right now, but don't you think he will eventually? And be angry? What will I do then, Nora? How can I justify what I did?"

"I don't know. What I do know is it's counterproductive to worry about things you can't control. If the worst happens, you'll deal with it. And I still say you have a great relationship with your son, and I think that will win out in the end."

"I hope you're right. I really hope you're right. Because I can't lose him, Nora. That would kill me."

Stephen called Elliott when he was about thirty minutes from High Creek. He could hear noises in the background and knew Elliott was in the stable. "Just thought I'd let you know I'm on my way home."

"Good trip?"

"Very good."

"Where'd you end up going?"

"To Austin."

"Did you by any chance see Jill and Jordan while you were there?"

"Yes, I did. If this isn't a bad time, I'll come out to the ranch and tell you about it."

"Great."

Stephen had rehearsed what he'd say and how he'd say it, but when he saw Elliott, he realized once again that it wouldn't be easy. The brothers walked over to the paddock area where they'd have some privacy. Stephen's stomach was tied in knots and he said a silent prayer that he could do this without upsetting or hurting Elliott any more than necessary.

"Is Jill doing all right?" Elliott asked. His eyes, so like their mother's, held genuine concern.

"She's lost a bit of weight. Other than that, she seems okay."

"And Jordan? How'd he look?"

"That's another story. He's been upset. But you knew that from his phone calls."

Elliott nodded.

"He was disappointed you weren't with me."

Elliott smiled. "He's such a great kid. I really miss him. Did you talk to Jill about him coming to visit?"

"I did. And she's agreeable."

"Good."

"I took him out riding yesterday. He said to tell you he's getting really good."

Elliott grinned. "And is he?"

"He's a natural, in my opinion."

They lapsed into silence then, each lost in his own thoughts. The sounds of the ranch surrounded them. Ordinary sounds. Too ordinary for what Stephen had to say. Taking a deep breath, he knew he couldn't postpone the moment of truth any longer. "There's something I need to tell you, Elliott."

Elliott turned to look at him. His expression was curious but there was no sense of alarm.

"I should have told you some of this weeks ago. I wish I had. I'm sorry that I didn't."

Now Elliott's forehead creased in a puzzled frown. "What are you talking about?"

"It's…about Jill. Jill and Jordan."

The frown became deeper. "What about them?"

Stephen looked down. Then slowly, he raised his eyes to meet Elliott's. "This will come as a shock, and I'm sorry about that. When you brought Jill to the ranch, it…it wasn't the first time I'd seen her."

"What?"

"She and I met years ago. I recognized her immediately and she recognized me."

Elliott simply stared.

"I was in my senior year of college at Harvard. She was a sophomore in college then, just nineteen. We were both at Padre Island for spring break. That's how we met."

"You *knew* each other? Why didn't you say something?"

"Because…" *Damn. It was even harder to say the words than he'd imagined it would be.* "Because we were more than casual acquaintants. We…" He swallowed. "We were lovers."

Elliott's mouth dropped open, and for a moment he didn't say anything. "Lovers!" He shook his head as if he didn't believe what Stephen had just said.

"It was just one of those things. We were kids. It was a summer romance. It only lasted five days. Then she left and I forgot all about her." *Well, that part wasn't strictly true, but it was close enough to the truth.*

Elliott still looked stunned. "Lovers," he said again. "You and Jill."

Stephen nodded.

"And you… Neither of you said a word."

"I was too shocked to say anything. So was she. Hell, Elliott, she was your *fiancée*. It was surreal. I couldn't believe it. Neither of us knew what to say. You sure don't expect to meet an old lover under those circumstances."

"So you and Jill talked about it."

"Not at first. But after a week or so, I could see she was very uncomfortable and I sure was, so then we *did* talk about it, and…and we agreed not to say anything."

"Why not? Don't you think I had a right to know?"

Stephen heaved a sigh. "Yes, of course. But we were worried about how you'd take the news. I—I didn't want to hurt you, and Jill felt the same way."

"Jesus, Stephen."

"I'm sorry, Elliott. I know now we should have come clean."

"Yes, you should have." Elliott bowed his head. It was obvious he was deeply disturbed by Stephen's revelation.

Stephen wished with all his heart that he didn't have to tell his brother the rest. Taking another deep breath, he said quietly, "There's more."

Elliott looked up. "More."

Stephen nodded.

Suddenly Elliott's eyes widened. "Wait a minute. You met when she was nineteen, you say?"

"Yes." Stephen could almost see the wheels turning in Elliott's head. He knew the exact moment the whole truth jelled in his brother's mind.

"*You're* the reason Jill left. *You're* Jordan's father, aren't you?"

Stephen swallowed. "Yes. But I didn't know that until the day before she left the ranch. She didn't tell me, and even though I wondered, I figured it wasn't possible. You see, I thought Jordan was nine. It wasn't until you said something about his birthday that I put two and two together. I swear, Elliott. If I'd had any idea, I would have told you right away."

Elliott's eyes were so full of pain, Stephen could hardly bear to look at them. "And even after she left, you never said anything."

"I wanted to, but I couldn't! I had to talk to Jill first. I had to find out what she planned to do."

"About what?"

"About me. Whether she was going to let me be a part of Jordan's life…or not."

"I see."

Stephen couldn't stand the way Elliott was looking at him. Never before had his brother ever shown him anything but love and pride. But neither of those emotions was on his face today. Instead his expression was filled with disappointment and something else. Shame.

"Elliott, I'm so sorry. I can't tell you how sorry I am."

"You know, Stephen, right now I don't think I want to talk to you anymore." He started to walk away.

Stephen grabbed his arm. "Wait, Elliott, please don't go. We can't leave things like this. There are still some things we need to settle."

Elliott shook him off. "I told you. I don't feel like talking anymore. Right now all I want is to be alone."

Five minutes later, his truck went up the road in a cloud of dust.

Stephen couldn't sleep. At two a.m., exhausted from trying, he dragged himself out of bed and went out to his small kitchen where he put on a pot of coffee. If he was going to be sleepless, he might as well get something accomplished. He had a will and a prenup to write, so he'd get a head start on the day's work.

But three hours later, battling a raging headache, he still hadn't managed to get much work done because he couldn't concentrate. Instead his thoughts continued to go in circles, and the unanswered questions wouldn't leave him in peace.

Would things ever be the same between him and Elliott?

What was he going to do?

He wished he had someone he could talk to. But the only person who would understand, the only person who would sympathize, the only person he *wanted* to talk to was Jill. And talking to Jill was fraught with danger. In fact, he wasn't sure how he was going to maintain the kind of relationship he wanted with Jordan. Seeing Jordan would mean seeing Jill. And each time Stephen saw Jill, his feelings for her grew harder to hide.

Downing two Advil tablets, he tried not to think about how she'd looked the other night. God, when they'd stood in her driveway after he'd followed her home, he had wanted to kiss her so badly he wasn't sure he would be able to stop himself. Yet somehow he had. Of course, he thought wryly, it had helped that she'd fled into the house before he could act on his impulses.

That alone—her running away—had told him she felt the same way he did. Neither of them seemed able to control themselves when they were together. At least, not for long. Sooner or later the attraction that had always simmered between them boiled over.

How did I end up in this mess?

More to the point, how was he going to resolve it? Because right now, Stephen could see no way at all that things between him and Jill could ever work out.

Stephen had the shower on full blast and was washing his hair when he thought he heard his phone ringing. He shut off the water and opened the shower door. That wasn't the phone. It was the doorbell. Who the hell could *that* be at this hour of the morning? It wasn't even seven o'clock yet.

Swearing, he grabbed a towel and wrapped it around him, then—trailing water and dripping shampoo all over his hardwood floors—he stalked to the door and looked out.

It was Elliott!

Stephen flung the door open. "C'mon in. I've gotta rinse off. I'll be right back." Not waiting to see if his brother complied, he hurried back to the bathroom.

Five minutes later, rinsed, dried off and dressed in clean jeans and a cotton T-shirt, Stephen padded barefoot into the living room where Elliott was sitting, just staring into space. He looked like Stephen had felt before the shower and the Advil.

"Want some coffee?" Stephen said.

Bloodshot eyes turned his way. "I've been drinking coffee since four o'clock. I think I'm coffeed out."

Stephen nodded and sank into a chair. "Yeah. I had a bad night, too."

Elliott leaned forward. "What are we going to do about this?"

"What do you want to do?"

"What I want is for everything to be the way it's always been." He grimaced. "But that's not going to happen."

"No." Stephen ached for his brother. He ached for himself. Hell, he ached for everyone concerned.

"Tell me something," Elliott said. "Are you in love with Jill?"

Stephen's heart skipped. This, he knew, was probably the defining moment of his relationship with Elliott. "Yes, I am."

"And does she feel the same way?"

"I don't know. We haven't talked about that."

Elliott nodded, then bowed his head.

The only sounds in the room were the ticking of the mantel clock and the distant hum of the refrigerator. Dust motes floated in the air, highlighted by the rays of morning sunlight that poured through the eastern windows. Time seemed to stand still. Stephen wanted to say more, wanted to try to explain, but pretty much everything had already been said.

Finally Elliott looked up. There was a hint of a smile on his face, and Stephen felt his first stirring of hope. "Okay," he said. "It may be awkward at first, but if you and Jill end up together, I think I can live with it." He stood.

Stephen jumped up. "Are you sure about this, Elliott?"

"Would it make any difference to you if I wasn't?"

"Of course it would."

"Does that mean you'd never act on the way you feel about Jill if I told you I couldn't handle it?"

Stephen slowly shook his head. "I'm not sure I could promise that. I don't seem able to help myself where she's concerned."

Now Elliott's smile, if not joyful, was at least genuine. "Good. Because she's worth whatever you have to give up to get her. And if you *didn't* feel that way about her, I'd say you didn't deserve her."

Chapter Sixteen

Jill had been going crazy wondering what had happened. She'd called Stephen's cell phone at least five times that morning and each time she'd gotten his voice mail. "Please call me," she'd begged. "I won't rest until I know what Elliott had to say."

In desperation she'd even called his office.

"I'm sorry, Miss Emerson," his secretary said, "but he's not here. He called early this morning and said he had something important to take care of and wouldn't be in today. If he calls in, I'll tell him you called, though."

Jill wanted to scream.

Why hadn't Stephen called her? Maybe something had happened and he wasn't able to talk to Elliott yesterday. Or maybe he *had* talked to him and Elliott hadn't taken the news well and Stephen didn't want to talk about it.

But surely, surely he'd call today.

Thank goodness Jordan wasn't home, she thought as she paced around and waited and hoped to hear from Stephen. The day he'd spent with Stephen seemed to have done her son a world of good and as a result he'd actually accepted his friend Kevin's invitation to go to a local water park today and, miracle of miracles, to spend the night tonight.

So Jill had an entire day free to paint. Normally she'd have been thrilled. Ecstatic even. But because she was so worried about what had happened between Stephen and Elliott and how that would impact all of them, she couldn't settle down enough to get any work done.

If only Stephen would call….

She decided she would work out her frustration on the treadmill. After changing into workout clothes—shorts, a tank top, socks and her Adidas—she grabbed her cell and her headphones and headed for the back bedroom where her treadmill cohabited with her sewing machine, her ironing board and a myriad of junk she should probably try to sell in a garage sale one of these days.

Walking briskly to dance music by Gwen Stefani, she managed to work up a sweat and temporarily, at least, forget about her troubles. By the time she'd finished, forty-five minutes later, she felt ten times better. But she was in dire need of a shower, which was problematic. With her luck, Stephen would probably call her back then.

Still…she'd have to chance it. Taking off the headphones, she grabbed her cell and headed for the bathroom, where she took the fastest shower on record.

She was in the middle of dressing when the doorbell rang. Oh, shoot. It was probably some sales type, even though there were signs clearly posted in her subdivision prohibiting door-to-door solicitations. Yet they continued to come. She felt like ignoring the bell. But whoever it was was persistent, because the doorbell rang again and then a third time.

"Okay," she muttered as she hurriedly pulled a clean T-shirt out of a drawer and drew it over her still-wet head. "I'm coming. But if you're selling something, you are in big trouble."

Her heart leaped into her throat when she looked through the peephole, because it was not a sales type standing on her stoop. It was Stephen. In the flesh.

"Stephen!" she said as she yanked open the door. "I've been waiting for you to call me!" Distractedly, she realized how she looked: no makeup, wet hair, bare feet.

He had the oddest look on his face as he stepped inside, closing the door behind him.

"What is it?" she said in alarm. "Did you talk to Elliott?"

"Yes, and I'll tell you all about it, but first I have two questions." His eyes pinned hers.

A woman could drown in his eyes, she thought. She shivered. "W-what?" she whispered.

"Where's Jordan?"

"He's not here. He's gone for the day."

"Good. Second question. Do you love me?"

That question took her so by surprise, she actually stumbled back as if he'd struck her. Her heart thudded in her ears.

Reaching for her, he placed his hands on her shoulders. "I love *you,* Jill. And I need to know if you feel the same way."

She wanted to say no. No was the safe answer. But

she couldn't lie to him. Not any more. Tears welled in her eyes. "Yes. I love you. But—"

Cutting off her words, he began kissing her. Kissing her as if he could never get enough of her. Kissing her lips, her eyes, her nose. Burying his hands in her hair. Kissing her and kissing her. And in between, murmuring her name again and again.

Still kissing her, he walked her back to the family room. And there, in the bright, warm sunlight, he undressed her and in between, managed to divest himself of his own clothes.

"Stephen…" But whatever she'd been going to say was lost in the sensations roaring through her.

"God, you're beautiful," he said. And then he was kissing her everywhere, his mouth trailing over her body, his hands finding all the places that remembered him.

Eventually, they moved into Jill's bedroom, where their lovemaking built in intensity. Stephen was a wonderful lover, thoughtful and generous. He seemed to know exactly what would please her and how to make her shiver and moan and cry out.

In return, she relearned the planes and muscles of his body—the hard places as well as the soft places. Soon she lost whatever reticence she might have had and loved him with abandon, rediscovering the joy of making love.

When he finally entered her she was more than ready for him—wet, hot and quivering with need. Feeling him inside, going deeper and deeper, she knew this was where she belonged. Where she'd always belonged. She wound her legs around him and lifted herself to meet him. Within minutes, great, shuddering waves of pleasure, so intense they were almost painful, engulfed her. And as they did, he cried out and with one last hard thrust, emptied into her.

A long time later, lying together in Jill's bed, Stephen finally told her about his two conversations with Elliott.

Jill began to cry when he told her what Elliott had said right before Stephen left him early that morning. "I'm the one who never deserved *him*."

Stephen gently wiped her tears away with his thumb. "He doesn't feel that way. He wants you to be happy."

But all Jill could think about was how good to her Elliott had been. And how she'd repaid him by hurting him.

"Jill…"

Jill looked into Stephen's eyes.

"Will you marry me?"

"M-marry you?"

He smiled. "That's what I said."

"And…and come back to High Creek?"

"And come back to High Creek."

"B-but maybe Elliott won't be able to handle *that*."

"I think he will. But if he can't, then we'll live somewhere else. Shoot, I could live here. I've always liked Austin. Luckily, money's not a problem. But we both know Jordan would be a lot happier in High Creek, close to the ranch. And I think Elliott would be, too. Of course, if we stay there, it means you'd have to quit your job again."

Jill's mind was spinning. She was filled with doubts, yet she was excited, too. The thought of marrying Stephen and living in High Creek filled her with a lightness she hadn't experienced since she was a kid.

"What do you say? Do I have to get down on one

knee? I know I have to get you a ring, but I can't wait that long for an answer. I've lost too much time without you and our son already."

Looking into his eyes—this love of her life—all her doubts were swept away. Yes, they had problems. But together they would face them and together they would overcome them. She smiled and touched Stephen's face tenderly. "I love you, Stephen. And yes, I'll marry you."

They spent the rest of the day and half the night talking, in between making love again, foraging in the kitchen for something to eat, showering together and making love some more.

"I don't think I'll ever get tired of making love with you," Stephen said.

"You say that now, but wait till I'm old and wrinkled," Jill said, laughing.

"I'll be older and more wrinkled, so it won't matter."

But the teasing and lovemaking came to an end the following morning when it was time for Jordan to come home. Jill had promised Kevin's mother that she would pick him up.

"I'm coming with you," Stephen said.

Jordan's eyes lit up when he saw Stephen. "Stephen! I didn't know you were gonna be here again."

"I didn't, either, son. But I wanted to see your mom and talk to you. We both want to talk to you."

"What about?"

"Let's go home first," Jill said. "And we'll talk there, okay?"

"Okay."

Thank goodness the drive only took ten minutes, Jill

thought. She knew she could not change the outcome of Jordan's reaction, no matter *how* he felt, so it was pointless to worry, but she couldn't stop.

They sat at the kitchen table. They'd agreed ahead of time that Stephen would initiate the conversation.

"What we wanted to talk to you about is your father," Stephen said.

Jordan frowned. "My father?"

"Yes. Your mom tells me that in the past you've been curious about him."

Jordan shrugged. "Yeah, I guess so." But he wasn't as disinterested as he acted. His eyes gave him away; they were bright and intent.

"What if I told you that you already know your father?"

Jordan's eyes widened.

Stephen reached across and clasped Jordan's hand. "Son, I'm your father."

"My…my *real* father?" Jordan squeaked.

"Yes."

"But…" Jordan looked at Jill.

Jill kept her trembling hands in her lap.

"You told me you didn't know where my father was!"

"I know I did, honey. And when I told you that, it was true."

Jordan's brilliant blue eyes met Stephen's. "Are you *really* my father?"

"Yes, son, I am."

The smile that illuminated Jordan's face put a lump in Jill's throat.

Now Stephen reached for her hand. "And your mom and I are going to get married so the three of us can live together and be a family."

"Yes!" Jordan punched the air with his free hand. "Can we go back to the ranch now?"

"Jordan," Jill cautioned. "We're not going to be living on the ranch. We'll probably be living in High Creek. In Stephen's house."

"That's okay," Jordan said. "I like it there, too. It's gonna be so *great* to be a family. And we can go out to the ranch to ride and so I can help Antonio, right?"

"Right," Stephen said.

Jill could no longer hold back her tears. But they were tears of happiness. Stephen's eyes were suspiciously shiny, too.

At that moment, her heart was so full, she thought it might burst. Now the only thing left for her to want was Elliott's happiness. And she would pray every single day that he would find it, just as they had.

Later, after Jordan had gone to bed, starry-eyed because they'd told him the three of them would drive out to the ranch in the morning, Stephen said, "I don't want you to worry, Jill. Elliott will be fine with this, I'm sure of it."

"But if he isn't?"

"If he isn't, then we'll do what I said. I'll move up here. We'll find some land nearby and build a house and a place to keep a couple of horses."

"And what about your law practice?"

"I can practice law anywhere in Texas, you know that."

"But—"

He put his arms around her, held her close. "We're so lucky to have found each other again. Nothing is going to spoil that."

"But the last thing I ever wanted was to come

between you and Elliott." Jill couldn't stand the thought that their relationship might be forever damaged because of her.

"I know."

"He means so much to you. And you mean so much to him."

Stephen drew back so that he could look at her. "Now listen, Jill, and listen good. Yes, Elliott means a lot to me. And I hope we will always be close. But you and Jordan mean even more. I'll be sad if Elliott has a problem with us being married, but it won't stop me. Because now that I've found you again, I'm never letting you go."

His kiss said it even more eloquently than his words.

And for the first time since that fateful night at the ranch when Jill recognized Stephen, she actually believed that the three of them could look forward to a happy, bright future together.

Epilogue

Three years later...

"I think Christmas weddings are so romantic, don't you?"

Jill looked at Nora and smiled. "Oh, I don't know," she said, thinking of her own wedding. "I'm kind of partial to autumn weddings, myself." Her gaze moved to Stephen, who as Elliott's best man, was standing behind his brother as they waited for the music to begin and for Elliott's bride to enter the room.

Stephen winked at her.

Love filled her heart. God had been so good to them, much more generous than she deserved. Every day she thanked him for the blessings he'd bestowed. She thought about how understanding Elliott had been. How he'd wholeheartedly welcomed her into the family as Stephen's wife. How he'd never made her feel bad about anything that had happened. How thrilled he'd been when Hannah was born. Almost as thrilled and she and Stephen were.

Jill touched her slightly rounded stomach. And in five months, the Wells family would welcome yet another child.

Beside her, Jordan was whispering to his sister, who was sitting on his lap. Hannah was the most stubborn two-year-old imaginable. She adored her big brother and had insisted that no one but him could hold her today.

She'd pushed Jill away, sticking out her bottom lip and saying, "No, no." *No* was her favorite word. "Jo-dan hold me!" Hannah had a problem with the name Jordan, so Jo-dan it was. Today she looked adorable in a green velvet dress and sparkly gold Mary Janes. She was very proud of the shoes. Even now she stuck them out in front of her and grinned as she saw Jill watching her. Jill leaned over and kissed her children, then shushed Hannah, who was now beginning to fidget.

Once she quieted down again, Jill glanced around. She wondered what Caroline was thinking today. Jill's one regret about becoming a member of Stephen's family was her continuing cool relationship with Caroline. Jill had tried. She'd tried mightily, in fact, but Caroline continued to keep her at arm's length. At least Elliott's daughter was no longer openly hostile. And thank goodness, she seemed to get along with Charlie. Jill guessed that was as much as anyone could hope for.

Just then the organist began to play "Trumpet Volun-

tary." At the sound, the guests in the small Congrega-
tional church turned as if one collective body.

Jill smiled as Charlie's granddaughter, Madison,
adorable in red velvet ballet slippers and a white lace
dress with a red velvet sash, began to walk down the aisle,
tossing rose petals in her wake. After her came Charlie's
daughter, Michelle, followed by her other daughter,
Megan—Madison's mother—who was the matron of
honor. The two young women wore long red satin dresses
and carried small bouquets of white orchids.

When Charlie came into view, there were oohs and
aahs from the guests. She did look gorgeous, Jill
thought. Her long sheath gown was also white lace,
which was extremely complimentary to her dark hair,
and she carried a cascade of red roses festooned with
silver ribbon.

"I think it's perfectly all right to wear white even if
I *have* been married before," she'd said.

Jill had agreed with her.

Turning her attention back to the altar, Jill studied
Elliott as he watched Charlie's approach. He looked so
happy today. All the sadness was gone from his eyes,
and now they were shining and filled with love. Jill still
couldn't believe the miracle of him and Charlie, but she
was thrilled they'd found each other.

Charlie reached the altar and Elliott moved forward.
For a moment, the two clasped hands and gazed into
each other's eyes.

"Dearly beloved, we are gathered here today…" the
minister began.

As Jill listened to the beautiful words, her heart felt so
full. Once again, Stephen glanced her way. As their eyes

met, Jill wished she could capture this magical moment forever. Sitting here in this beautiful little church, surrounded by all the people she loved, taking part in this wonderful day, anticipating the birth of yet another beloved child... Who could ask for anything more?

Mrs. Stephen Wells, she told herself, *you are the luckiest woman in the world.*

* * * * *

Celebrate 60 years of pure reading pleasure with Harlequin!

To commemorate the event, Harlequin Intrigue® is thrilled to invite you to the wedding of The Colby Agency's J. T. Baxley and his bride, Eve Mattson.

That is, of course, if J.T. can find the woman who left him at the altar. Considering he's a private investigator for one of the top agencies in the country—the best of the best—that shouldn't be a problem. The real setback is that his bride isn't who she appears to be…and her mysterious past has put them both in danger.

Enjoy an exclusive glimpse of Debra Webb's latest addition to
THE COLBY AGENCY:
ELITE RECONNAISSANCE DIVISION

THE BRIDE'S SECRETS

Available August 2009 from Harlequin Intrigue®.

The dark figures on the dock were still firing. The bullets cutting through the surface of the water without the warning boom of shots told Eve they were using silencers.

That was to her benefit. Silencers decreased the accuracy of every shot and lessened the range.

She grabbed for the rocks. Scrambled through the darkness. Bumped her knee on a boulder. Cursed.

Burrowing into the waist-deep grass, she kept low and crawled forward. Faster. Pushed harder. Needed as much distance as possible.

Shots pinged on the rocks.

J.T. scrambled alongside her.

He was breathing hard.

They had to stay close to the ground until they reached the next row of warehouses. Even though she was relatively certain they were out of range at this point, she wasn't taking any risks. And she wasn't slowing down.

J.T. had to keep up.

The splat of a bullet hitting the ground next to Eve had her rolling left. Maybe they weren't completely out of range.

She bumped J.T. He grunted.

His injured arm. Dammit. She could apologize later.

Half a dozen more yards.

Almost in the clear.

As she reached the cover of the alley between the first two warehouses she tensed.

Silence.

No pings or splats.

She glanced back at the dock. Deserted.

Time to run.

Her car was parked another block down.

Pushing to her feet, she sprinted forward. The wet bag dragged at her shoulder. She ignored it.

By the time she reached the lot where her car was parked, she had dug the keys from her pocket and hit the fob. Six seconds later she was behind the wheel. She hit the ignition as J.T. collapsed into the passenger seat. Tires squealed as she spun out of the slot.

"What the hell did you do to me?"

From the corner of her eye she watched him shake his head in an attempt to clear it.

He would be pissed when she told him about the tranquilizer.

She'd needed him cooperative until she formulated a plan. A drug-induced state of unconsciousness had been the fastest and most efficient method to ensure his continued solidarity.

"I can't really talk right now." Eve wove into the right lane as the street widened to four lanes. What she needed was traffic. It was Saturday night—shouldn't be that difficult to find as soon as they were out of the old warehouse district.

A glance in the rearview mirror warned that their unwanted company had caught up.

Sensing her tension, J.T. turned to peer over his left shoulder.

"I hope you have a plan B."

She shot him a look. "There's always plan G." Then she pulled the Glock out of her waistband.

Cutting the steering wheel left, she slid between two vehicles. Another veer to the right and she'd put several cars between hers and the enemy.

She was betting they wouldn't pull out the firepower in the open like this, but a girl could never be too sure when it came to an unknown enemy.

Deep blending was the way to go.

Two traffic lights ahead, the marquis of a movie theater provided exactly the opportunity she was looking for.

The digital numbers on the dash indicated it was just past midnight. Perfect timing. The late movie would be purging its audience into the crowd of teenagers who liked hanging out in the parking lot.

She took a hard right onto the property that sported a twelve-screen theater, numerous fast-food hot spots and a chain superstore. Speeding across the lot, she selected a lane of parking slots. Pulling in as close to the theater entrance as possible, she shut off the engine and reached for her door.

"Let's go."

Thankfully he didn't argue.

Rounding the hood of her car, she shoved the Glock into her bag, then wrapped her arm around J.T.'s and merged into the crowd.

With her free hand she finger-combed her long hair. It was soaked, as were her clothes. The kids she bumped into noticed, gave her death-ray glares.

They just didn't know.

As she and J.T. moved in closer to the building, she grabbed a baseball cap from an innocent bystander. The crowd made it easy. The kid who owned the cap had made it even easier by stuffing the cap bill-first into his waistband at the small of his back.

Pushing through the loitering crowd, she made her way to the side of the building next to the main entrance. She pushed J.T. against the wall and dropped her bag to the ground. Peeled off her T-shirt and let it fall.

His gaze instantly zeroed in on her breasts, where the cami she wore had glued to her skin like an extra layer. A zing of desire shot through her veins.

Not the time.

With a flick of her wrist she twisted her hair up and clamped the cap atop the blond mass.

"They're coming," J.T. muttered as he gazed at some point beyond her.

"Yeah, I know." She planted her palms against the wall on either side of him and leaned in. "Keep your eyes open. Let me know when they're inside."

Then she planted her lips on his.

* * * * *

Will J.T. and Eve be caught in the moment?
Or will Eve get the chance to reveal all of her secrets?
Find out in
THE BRIDE'S SECRETS
by Debra Webb.
Available August 2009 from Harlequin Intrigue®.

We'll be spotlighting a different series every month
throughout 2009 to celebrate our 60th anniversary.

LOOK FOR
HARLEQUIN INTRIGUE®
IN AUGUST!

To commemorate the event, Harlequin Intrigue® is thrilled
to invite you to the wedding of the Colby Agency's
J. T. Baxley and his bride, Eve Mattson.

Look for *Colby Agency: Elite Reconnaissance*

THE BRIDE'S SECRETS
BY DEBRA WEBB

Available August 2009

www.eHarlequin.com

REQUEST YOUR FREE BOOKS!

2 FREE NOVELS PLUS 2 FREE GIFTS!

SPECIAL EDITION®

Life, Love and Family!

YES! Please send me 2 FREE Silhouette Special Edition® novels and my 2 FREE gifts (gifts are worth about $10). After receiving them, if I don't wish to receive any more books, I can return the shipping statement marked "cancel." If I don't cancel, I will receive 6 brand-new novels every month and be billed just $4.24 per book in the U.S. or $4.99 per book in Canada. That's a savings of at least 15% off the cover price! It's quite a bargain! Shipping and handling is just 50¢ per book.* I understand that accepting the 2 free books and gifts places me under no obligation to buy anything. I can always return a shipment and cancel at any time. Even if I never buy another book from Silhouette, the two free books and gifts are mine to keep forever.

235 SDN EYN4 335 SDN EYPG

Name	(PLEASE PRINT)

Address	Apt. #

City	State/Prov.	Zip/Postal Code

Signature (if under 18, a parent or guardian must sign)

Mail to the Silhouette Reader Service:
IN U.S.A.: P.O. Box 1867, Buffalo, NY 14240-1867
IN CANADA: P.O. Box 609, Fort Erie, Ontario L2A 5X3

Not valid to current subscribers of Silhouette Special Edition books.

Want to try two free books from another line?
Call 1-800-873-8635 or visit www.morefreebooks.com.

* Terms and prices subject to change without notice. Prices do not include applicable taxes. Sales tax applicable in N.Y. Canadian residents will be charged applicable provincial taxes and GST. Offer not valid in Quebec. This offer is limited to one order per household. All orders subject to approval. Credit or debit balances in a customer's account(s) may be offset by any other outstanding balance owed by or to the customer. Please allow 4 to 6 weeks for delivery. Offer available while quantities last.

Your Privacy: Silhouette is committed to protecting your privacy. Our Privacy Policy is available online at www.eHarlequin.com or upon request from the Reader Service. From time to time we make our lists of customers available to reputable third parties who may have a product or service of interest to you. If you would prefer we not share your name and address, please check here. ☐

SSE09R

COMING NEXT MONTH
Available July 28, 2009

#1987 THE TEXAS BODYGUARD'S PROPOSAL—
Karen Rose Smith
The Foleys and the McCords
Burned by her Greek tycoon ex, supermodel Gabby McCord
sought refuge in her work on the glitzy PR campaign for her
family's retail jewelry empire. Finding refuge in the arms of new
bodyguard Rafael Balthazar was an unexpected perk!

#1988 FROM FRIENDS TO FOREVER—Karen Templeton
Guys and Daughters
Widowed coach Tony Vaccaro had his hands full raising his three
daughters, so it was *really* inconvenient when old friend Lili Szabo
came back to town and a teenage crush was reignited. Then they
stole one night for themselves, and life changed...forever.

#1989 RACE TO THE ALTAR—Judy Duarte
Brighton Valley Medical Center
When race car driver Chase Mayfield's fast life landed him in the
hospital, nurse Molly Chambers was there to bring him back from
the edge. But after a night of passion had unintended consequences,
would Chase be there for her?

#1990 DIAGNOSIS: DADDY—Gina Wilkins
Doctors in Training
For med student Connor Hayes, taking custody of the daughter
he'd never known was tough. Would he have to drop out? Not
with longtime friend Mia Doyle there to help. But was Mia up to
multitasking as best friend, nanny...and love of Connor's life?

#1991 SEVENTH BRIDE, SEVENTH BROTHER—
Nicole Foster
The Brothers of Rancho Pintada
Coming home was hell for prodigal daughter turned social worker
Risa Charez. Until she met Ry Kincaid. The gruff but tender loner,
a long-lost Rancho Pintada brother, was new to town, new at love...
and definitely unprepared for Risa's explosive secret.

#1992 ONCE UPON A WEDDING—Stacy Connelly
Party planner Kelsey Wilson was rolling out all the stops for her
cousin's wedding. But meddlesome P.I. Connor McClane wanted to
put a stop to the affair. The more they clashed, the more they realized
their own nuptials could be looming on the horizon!

SSECNMBPA0709